"Red is the colour of desire."

Morgan drawled the words softly, intimately. Kathleen felt her skin prickle as if he'd physically caressed her.

"I beg your pardon?" she said crisply, trying to fend off their effect.

He smiled for the first time—a white, dazzling flash that was both wicked and knowing—sending a weird shock wave through Kathleen's heart. He gave a soft little laugh and strolled toward her.

"Red and black...opposing forces...that is what we are...thrown together against our own personal inclinations. Yet who is to say what might not be created, or whose purpose is best served? Yours...mine...ours."

He trailed his fingers through her hair. "You should always wear your hair like this. It's beautiful. And with the pure contrast of your voice...the promise of fire and passion...what might we not weave together?"

EMMA DARCY nearly became an actress until her fiancé declared he preferred to attend the theater *with* her. She became a wife and mother. Later she took up oil painting—unsuccessfully, she remarks. Then, she tried architecture, designing the family home in New South Wales. Next came romance writing—"the hardest and most challenging of all the activities," she confesses.

Books by Emma Darcy

EMMA DARCY

the colour of desire

Harlequin Books

**TORONTO • NEW YORK • LONDON
AMSTERDAM • PARIS • SYDNEY • HAMBURG
STOCKHOLM • ATHENS • TOKYO • MILAN**

This book is dedicated to Jacqui Bianchi—
for all she taught us
and all she shared with us.
Vale Jacqui!
We will always remember you.

Harlequin Presents first edition August 1991
ISBN 0-373-11385-4

Original hardcover edition published in 1990
by Mills & Boon Limited

THE COLOUR OF DESIRE

CHAPTER ONE

'QUICKLY now, Kathleen. The car is here. There's no time to waste.'

Kathleen Mavourney set aside the music sheets she had been sorting through and picked up her handbag. The authority in Sister Cecily's voice automatically drew obedience. But the words compounded the curiosity that the elderly nun's uncharacteristic edginess had been stirring in Kathleen all morning.

'Where are we going?' she asked.

'Never mind that,' Sister Cecily said testily. She grabbed Kathleen's arm and bustled her down the corridor which linked the music wing to the much older structure of the convent proper.

Kathleen held her tongue. Tension emanated from the little woman and the strained look on her usually serene face did not invite questions. Now that they were actually on their way, undoubtedly this mystery outing would be explained soon enough. However, Kathleen's blue eyes widened in astonishment as Sister Cecily paused and picked up the violin case resting against the wall near the front door. The unusual instantly zoomed into the unbelievable!

'You're going to play somewhere, Sister?'

The incredulous question was only answered by a look of steely determination. The old nun opened the door and ushered Kathleen outside. Any more questions were temporarily knocked clear out of Kathleen's mind. Beyond the convent gates sat a black Rolls-Royce. A smartly uniformed chauffeur stood at attention near the passenger door. The moment he saw them coming he swung into action, leaving no doubt whatsoever that the car was here for them.

It was not until they were inside the Rolls and it was pulling away from the kerb that Kathleen recovered enough from the idea of riding in such state to look searchingly at the nun beside her.

Sister Mary Cecily was not an impressive figure of a woman. She was a head shorter than Kathleen—barely five feet tall—and stout. Her chubby face had few lines, despite the wearing of almost sixty years. In recent months she had not looked so well. There had been a grey look about her face which had perturbed Kathleen. But she had said there was nothing the matter with her, and right at this moment the smooth cheeks were looking particularly pink, and the light green eyes behind the gold-rimmed glasses held a definite gleam of satisfaction.

She leaned over and patted Kathleen's hand. 'It's all right, dear. I didn't tell you anything before because I was worried that he might not keep his word. But he has. And now it's up to you.'

'Sister, you're talking in riddles,' Kathleen said, shaking her head in confusion. 'What's up to me? And who does this car belong to? And where. . .?'

The nun smiled serenely. 'This is all about power, Kathleen. Power and influence. I've sown what seeds I can, and today. . .today I flex my muscles.'

The mental image of little Sister Cecily flexing her muscles brought a smile to Kathleen's lips, but any sense of whimsy was totally obliterated by the nun's next words.

'I'm taking you for an audition. You will sing "L'Absence" and I will accompany you on the violin, just as we have practised it. And you will be listened to as you deserve to be.'

Kathleen's throat instantly constricted. She stared in horror at the nun, at the violin case on the seat beside her, then shook her head in pained protest, too shocked and distressed to speak the wretched truth which made any audition futile. Besides, Sister Cecily knew it. She knew it as well as Kathleen did, and how she could blindly ignore it——

'Kathleen, I cannot teach you any more. You've got beyond what I know.' There was a tired inevitability in her tone that precluded any argument. The green eyes lit with a feverish purpose that held a measure of desperation. She took Kathleen's hand and squeezed it hard. 'This is the one chance I can give you for the kind of life you should have. You must seize it, my dear. You will get no other.'

Kathleen swallowed hard and tried to ignore the ache in her heart. 'Sister, you know it's an impossible dream. You've been so kind to. . .to keep on teaching me. But you know what I was told. There's no point. . .'

'There is point!' the nun scorned. 'You are never to give up, Kathleen Mavourney! All my life I have striven for perfection. I've never been content with less. Don't *you* ever be content with less either. You still have much to learn. And you must learn! Even if it is only to satisfy your own soul that you have given of your utmost, you must pursue the goal of perfection.'

Her voice slipped from the strident tone of a demanding teacher into the softer, infinitely more touching words of a personal friend. 'Of all the pupils I've had over the years there have been so few with the seed of greatness in them. You are one of them. Don't disappoint me, Kathleen Mavourney. Don't fail the faith I have in you.'

Tears pricked Kathleen's eyes and she barely held them in check as she turned her head away to stare blindly out of the window. Her own disappointment was a constant grief inside her but she had done her best to come to terms with it. Teaching music was all she was good for now, and teaching at the convent was the only way she could repay the nuns for all they had done for her when she had been crippled. Although, if she was completely honest with herself, it was always important to her to stay with Sister Cecily, perhaps because she was the one person who completely believed in her.

The train crash that had killed her parents had also shattered Kathleen's dream of becoming the best operatic soprano ever to grace the stage. Despite all the operations, and the miracle of being able to walk again, the injury to her knees had been so severe that her legs would never be strong enough to support her through a live performance—she had to accept that— but she couldn't bear to give up singing.

To hear her own voice developing, reaching and holding notes, mastering nuances of sound and subtle phrasing—the deep pleasure in achievement—the craving for perfection—she understood all too well that inner drive that Sister Cecily spoke about.

The wonderful little nun had indulged her need, guided her, driven her to reach deeper and deeper into herself to produce the sound, the intonation, the emotion, and had shared her joy in every improvement. But to go so far as to arrange an audition. . .surely she must realise it couldn't lead anywhere.

Many of the older nuns in the convent were very unworldly in their attitudes and beliefs. Kathleen had always believed Sister Cecily to be different, yet now it seemed that even she was letting her idealism push aside any sense of reality. And the stark practical reality was that even a successful audition could not achieve any change in Kathleen's circumstances.

As much as it pained her, she forced herself to point out the truth once more. 'Sister, I know you mean well, but have you told this person about my legs?'

'Kathleen!' Exasperation threaded her answer. 'They cannot be allowed to become an issue.'

'How can they not be an issue?' Kathleen cried in equal exasperation. 'You know that a scholarship, or any kind of patronage for further study, is invariably granted on the presumption that a promising career lies ahead; that there will eventually be a return for the investment made.'

'There will be a return! There has to be!' the little nun said determinedly.

'Sister! For heaven's sake! I haven't got the physical stamina to get through a full operatic performance. I can't even stand for any length of time without discomfort, let alone promise the kind of endurance necessary to carry out a professional schedule.'

'Maybe not,' came the imperturbable answer. A secretive little smile flitted over Sister Cecily's mouth. 'But please. . .no more of this defeatist talk. Something *will* come out of this audition.'

Kathleen knew that wasn't true. There was no hope. She had nursed a thin little hope that one day she might make it as a recording artist, but cold, hard reason told her it was only famous performing artists whom people wanted to hear, not someone who had never won any acclaim on a stage. As an unknown she would have no commercial value to any recording companies, no matter how good her voice was, and no matter how wonderfully she could interpret a song.

However, there was clearly no point in arguing any further. She had to go through with the audition, if only for Sister Cecily's sake. Obviously the arrangements had gone too far for her to back out now, but whatever the outcome she could only see the most painful embarrassment ahead for all parties involved.

The thought brought an inner agony of self-consciousness. This car had to belong to someone important, someone high up in the music world, and Sister Cecily's reference to 'he' meant it was a man. Someone of power and influence. Kathleen understood those words now, and writhed all the more on their account.

She would be wasting his time, whether he was impressed with her voice or not. And the man probably didn't want to listen to her at all. Sister Cecily had obviously pressed this favour from him, since she hadn't been sure whether he would keep his word or not.

Kathleen shrank even further inside herself. She didn't want to sing to him or for him. She didn't want to hear anything he had to say. She didn't want his criticisms, which he would undoubtedly have, since she was only twenty-one and relatively untrained for this kind of music. She certainly didn't want to know what might have been possible if the injury to her legs hadn't happened. It would only resharpen the frustration she had tried to bury.

Her fingers began a frantic pleating of her brown skirt. It was some considerable time before Kathleen became aware of the revealing action and consciously stopped it. A nervous little laugh almost erupted from her throat as she smoothed the practical tweed fabric. She was on her way to probably the only audition she would ever have in her life, and she wasn't even well dressed for it.

Plain brown homi-ped shoes on her feet; her legs encased in thick supportive tights; her brown skirt and fawn sweater totally unglamorous and not particularly flattering to her slender figure—even the somewhat startling cloud of red hair—the one really colourful feature in her whole appearance—was rolled into a French pleat, out of the way; and she hadn't bothered with any make-up—rarely did these days.

The fine smoothness of her complexion needed no masking but the paleness of her skin could have done with a touch-up of colour. And her over-generous mouth could have been played down a bit with a judicious use of lip-gloss. A coating of brown mascara on her thick red-gold lashes would have given some emphasis to the vivid blue of her eyes and a touch of pencil to highlight the arch of her eyebrows. . .

If only Sister Cecily had given her some warning. . .but the elderly nun wouldn't have seen anything amiss with Kathleen's appearance. Feminine vanity was not of her world and totally irrelevant anyway. An audition was an audition. Only the voice mattered. And of course she was right, Kathleen thought with dry irony. Except in this case, not even the voice mattered.

Kathleen didn't bother to press the unanswered question as to where they were going. That didn't matter either. But her curiosity was slightly piqued as the car moved smoothly towards the West End of London. When it slowed to a halt in front of the theatre where Morgan Llewellyn's latest musical had been playing for the past year she turned to Sister Cecily in frank puzzlement.

'Why are we stopping here?'

The light green eyes regarded her steadily, burning with a sense of mission that Kathleen could not grasp or understand. 'Morgan Llewellyn made that stipulation before he would agree to what I wanted. So I gave in to him that much. It's not perfect but it will have to do.'

Shock and incredulity almost strangled her voice again. 'Morgan Llewellyn is going to hear me sing?' she barely squeaked.

'Yes,' came the unperturbed reply.

The chauffeur was out, rounding the car to Sister Cecily's door. Confusion whirled through Kathleen's mind and a wild string of protests spilled from her lips. 'But why. . .why would he be interested in hearing me? It's not his kind of music. He writes something totally different. I couldn't do that sort of thing. I wouldn't want to. It's. . . I'm not in tune with his music scene at all. And besides, it's. . .it's just. . .'

Again Sister Cecily took her hand and pressed it hard, stilling its agitated fluttering. 'God works in mysterious ways. Sometimes I help Him with the obvious. After more than forty years in a convent, I know that, if you want certain things to happen, you must make them happen. You cannot always rely on things happening for the best. Today, I'm just giving events a little nudge. Trust me, Kathleen. And don't argue. It's one of your worst faults that you always want to argue. Try a little faith, my dear. Sing as I have taught you to sing. That's all you need to know. From there on in, events will unfold as they are meant to.'

The door was opened and she turned away to step out of the car, leaving Kathleen no alternative but to follow her. Her mind was in absolute chaos, her heart hammering madly against her ribs. This audition made no sense at all. Her kind of singing couldn't possibly appeal to Morgan Llewellyn. . .and what would he know about it? He was certainly at the top of the musical comedy field, but his work was a far cry from anything classical. His music was very modern and clever and witty, but Kathleen thought it rather empty. It very definitely wasn't the kind of music that enthralled her.

But she was given no time to sift through this absurd situation. They were met inside the theatre by a man who introduced himself as the stage manager. He ushered them through a series of corridors which led them inexorably towards the back of the theatre. Kathleen was virtually ignored. The manager addressed himself to Sister Cecily, taking objection to the violin case she carried.

'Mr Llewellyn called in the orchestra half an hour early for the matinee performance, especially to play for this audition, Sister. They're ready for you. They'll play any music you require,' he explained.

'No, they won't,' Sister Cecily replied firmly.

'Sister, they're familiar with all of Mr Llewellyn's songs. I assure you——'

'Kathleen will not be singing any of Morgan Llewellyn's work,' came the relentless reply.

The stage manager looked shocked. He rolled his eyes and shook his head. 'I hardly think that is going to please him, Sister.'

'Young man. . .' the manager was at least forty and a foot taller than Sister Cecily, but he might have been an insect under the sharp green glare of the nun's unshakeable authority '. . .if this audition were meant to please, it would serve no purpose at all. And if Morgan Llewellyn isn't bigger than that, I'll wipe my hands of him. I can't say I was ever that fond of him. He was never a good pupil. And I do not say that meanly. Generally speaking I prefer teaching boys: they're more adaptable.'

Which put the stage manager on about the same level of confusion that Kathleen was still suffering. He closed his mouth and said no more until he led them through the curtains and on to the apron of the stage. The orchestra was in the pit, warming up their instruments, and he moved forward to speak to the conductor.

Sister Cecily ignored them. She set about removing her violin from its case. Kathleen's heart felt as if it were being slowly squeezed in a vice. She was standing on a stage in a professional theatre, facing rows and rows of empty seats. This was probably the one and only time in her life she would occupy such a position, but it was not the place of her dreams.

In little more than an hour those seats would be filling for the Saturday matinee performance of Morgan Llewellyn's latest hit musical. Filling with people who wanted light musical entertainment, not classical artistry. It was all wrong for Kathleen to be here. And of Morgan Llewellyn himself there was no sign. Not that she knew what he looked like, but there was no one occupying any of the seats in front of her.

The conductor called up to Sister Cecily. 'Madam, what music do you require?'

'I don't require any,' Sister Cecily replied coolly. 'If you are asking what music I intend to play, it is the song 'L'Absence' from Berlioz's *Nuits d'été*.'

The noise from the orchestra pit ceased. Eyebrows were raised. Heads shook. The conductor made a helpless gesture at his musicians and turned to look up towards the centre of the mezzanine balcony.

'It seems we are not necessary. Do you have any instructions, Morgan?'

Kathleen made out a dark shape that looked as if it might be the person addressed. Only one thing was now clear in her mind. The favour of this audition had been given because Morgan Llewellyn had once been one of Sister Cecily's pupils, but what power and influence that old association carried still seemed to have no relevance to her own position.

After a short tense silence a voice replied—deep, hard, and curt in tone. 'Sit and listen. You might learn something.' Then the tone changed to one of dry resignation. 'If nothing else, you will certainly be treated to a virtuoso performance on the violin.'

It was small relief to know he had such deep respect for the nun who had taught him so many years ago. And was demanding respect from his orchestra too. But of course he had to respect Sister Cecily or he would never have agreed to this mad charade of an audition. Perhaps it was easier to indulge his former teacher than refuse her. Either way, it didn't make it any easier for Kathleen to accept the gross situation.

The stage manager offered Kathleen a microphone. Sister Cecily rejected it for her. A spotlight was turned on, dazzling her eyes and making her feel horribly exposed to the man who was watching up there in the darkness. Every nerve in her body was frozen. This was all so meaningless, pointless, mortifying.

The rustling of movement in the orchestra pit ceased. There was utter silence—waiting, listening silence. Yet what did any of it matter? Nothing hung in the balance. Nobody's opinion counted for anything here. . .except Sister Cecily's. She had to sing for her. . .not fail the faith she had in her.

And Morgan Llewellyn? He was only a name—a shape in the darkness—no one close—no one whose criticism would hurt, or whose acclaim would mean anything. He was a long way away from her. . .just as in the song she had to sing, the call to a beloved living somewhere far-off. . .so distant that there was never any chance of his answering.

The violin sang the haunting theme of the introduction under Sister Cecily's masterful touch. Kathleen took a deep breath and willed her vocal cords to produce the sound they had been taught, the trained purity of tone and cadence. And it came. . .that clear poignant call and its shaded echo. . .the sense of a loving heart in a desolate void.

Reviens, reviens. . .come back, come back. . .
Ma bien aimée. . .my beloved. . .

Again and again she sent it out until the last verse demanded the colourless tone of defeat. And Kathleen knew how to sing that. She felt it in every atom of her being. The last note drifted, lead-weighted, hopeless, unanswerable. . .into dead silence.

No one moved. No one applauded. Someone swore softly in the orchestra-pit. Whatever emotion he was expressing meant nothing to Kathleen. She didn't care. She had done what Sister Cecily had asked her to do to the best of her capability. Whatever happened now was irrelevant to her life. Even Morgan Llewellyn's reaction was irrelevant. With a sense of dull irony she realised that this was what everyone was waiting for.

They waited in vain. There was no discernible reaction from him. After several long moments of discomfiting silence, a barked order issued from the darkness. 'The orchestra is dismissed until the matinee call. Conduct Sister Cecily and her protégée to my office.'

The spotlight was turned off. The stage manager reappeared at Kathleen's side. There was restless movement and a low buzz of conversation from the orchestra pit. Sister Cecily calmly packed away her violin and walked over to Kathleen, wearing a smile of quiet satisfaction.

'It does not matter what Morgan says, Kathleen. Remember this. You can be proud of the way you sang just now. It was worthy of the gift God gave you.'

'Thank you, Sister,' Kathleen whispered. For some reason her throat had tightened up again at the thought of actually coming face to face with Morgan Llewellyn. He hadn't seemed quite real in the darkness. But the voice was real enough, and Kathleen felt she'd much prefer to keep the man behind that voice at a dark distance.

Sister Cecily heaved a tired sigh. 'And that's more than I can say of Morgan, despite all his successes. I hope and pray that. . .' She drew in a deep breath and patted Kathleen's hand. 'There is a chance. There has to be a chance. Leave everything to me, my dear. This is all about power. You are not to say anything.'

The stage manager cleared his throat and touched their arms to command their attention. 'If you'll come with me, ladies. . .'

Kathleen was conscious of the curious looks thrown at them by backstage staff as they made their way through the corridors again. No one—not even the stage manager—passed any audible comment on the audition. Which was perfectly understandable. One didn't expect to hear an operatic soprano singing classical music to a man who operated on a totally different level. They were probably all wondering what on earth was going on. Why it was even happening. Kathleen didn't know herself. The only person who could give an answer to that was Sister Mary Cecily, and she was keeping her own counsel.

Kathleen was working hard at inwardly dissociating

herself from the fast-approaching interview with Morgan Llewellyn. What Sister Cecily was hoping for from it she had no idea, and wasn't even sure if she wanted to know. Her talk of power made Kathleen very uneasy. She could foresee nothing but painful embarrassment.

The office they were shown into was nothing grand or intimidating. It contained a large workmanlike desk and several chairs, a row of filing cabinets along one wall, well-filled bookshelves along two others, and a large cabinet that Kathleen surmised contained the makings of convivial drinks—if the occasion warranted them. She suspected this one didn't.

The stage manager invited them to sit down and tactfully withdrew. Kathleen sat in the chair furthest from the desk. Sister Cecily wandered around scanning the contents of the bookshelves, her hands linked behind her back, fingers making agitated interlacing movements. She looked as tense as Kathleen felt.

Morgan Llewellyn didn't precisely explode into the room, yet, the moment he entered, his presence instantly dominated it. The air around him seemed to vibrate with a violent vitality. He was tall, aggressively masculine in form-fitting black clothes that clearly outlined his powerful physique. Thick black hair was sleekly styled to the sharp cut of his face which was strikingly individual—a broad brow, high prominent cheekbones, finely chiselled nose, a mouth that was more distinctly outlined than most, and an acute slash of the jawline to an uncompromising square chin. His eyes were hidden behind black sunglasses but Kathleen felt them flick at her like a whip-sting before he concentrated all his attention on the nun who had turned an incredibly serene face towards him.

'I will not mince words with you, Sister,' he said

curtly. 'I'm well aware of what you've been leading up to. But it will not work!'

He made a sharp dismissive gesture, stalked over to the desk, swung around, leaned back against it and folded his arms. The square chin lifted a fraction as he addressed Sister Cecily again, a cold pride slicing through every word.

'I suffered through your reading *Lorna Doone* to me while I was tied to that damned hospital bed. All six hundred and fifty-six interminable pages of that thoroughly boring old-fashioned book. I'll admit it served to distract me from worrying how much vision, if any, I would regain from the operation. I'll even concede that some parts of the story might be usable material.'

He paused for pointed emphasis. 'But your protégée is not—not by any stretch of the imagination—usable material! So, whatever you're asking, the answer is no. A categorical no!'

His head turned towards Kathleen, his face hard and forbidding. She wondered how much sight was hidden behind the dark glasses. He certainly had not moved like a blind man, and he had looked directly at both her and Sister Cecily.

'Whether you believe it or not,' he addressed her in a straightforward, unemotional tone, 'it is always much kinder to be cruelly blunt at the outset. It saves a great deal of unnecessary pain. You are not suited to my needs.'

He wasn't telling Kathleen anything startling or hurtful. She had known that before the audition. But it was certainly an experience to meet the man behind the name. He was nothing like what she might have expected—if she had ever stopped to think about him. However, before she could agree with his judgement,

Sister Cecily attacked both the judgement and the man
with mind-stunning ferocity.

'Then you are more blind, Morgan Llewellyn, than
I had ever thought possible!' Her voice carried a tone
of bitter disgust. 'Blinded by the glitter of the shallow
stream in which you have been so indolently swimming. Drowning your great talent! Taking the easy
path! Don't say I haven't warned you again and again.
I only wonder that you are not bored out of your mind
with what you're doing.'

He bared his teeth at her in anger. 'I am successful.
Many people would say very successful. And the
reason I am not bored with it, Sister, is that I am the
perfectionist you taught me to be. And there is a great
deal of satisfaction in getting the ultimate result from
any creative concept. Should I ever do *Lorna
Doone*. . .' he nodded towards Kathleen '. . . I would
never use her.'

'Are you deaf, Morgan Llewellyn?' Sister Cecily
taunted. 'Listen to the quality of the voice. Compose
for the voice. If you decide to do *Lorna Doone*. . .or
anything of true value and real emotion. . .create the
music for that voice and you will tear the hearts out of
your audience.'

Enlightenment burst through Kathleen's confusion.
As mad as it seemed, Sister Cecily believed that
Morgan Llewellyn could compose the kind of music
that would suit her voice and promote her into a
singing career. Apparently the little nun had been
working this angle for some time for Morgan Llewellyn
to be so angry about it.

His lips thinned in rigid rejection of the idea. 'You're
trying to bully me into doing what you want. And the
answer is no! No *Lorna Doone*! Certainly not your
way! No protégée your way! And there is no more to

be said! I'm going to give you a cheque for a thousand pounds to spend on your music wing at the convent. . .'

Sister Cecily moved, placing herself squarely in front of him, her short stout body held in lofty scorn. 'Money is not important, Morgan Llewellyn. And don't try to bribe me. You did it as a child, and you're still trying to do it now. Why are you so frightened of failing?'

He uncoiled his arms, straightened, every muscle in his body taut with power.

Kathleen's pulse was hammering in her ears. Her breath was trapped in her throat. She stared in mesmerised fascination at the two of them: the little bantam rooster of a nun relentlessly firing a barrage of criticism at a dangerous wolf of a man who looked as if he wanted to tear her to pieces.

'I'm not your pupil any more,' he said in a low threatening voice. 'I've carved my own path. I did it my way! As I've always done! And how I develop it is my business. I do not want your advice, nor anyone else's!'

'An infinite range of possibilities was yours, Morgan. You chose the least,' she retorted fearlessly. 'Face it. Change it. Before you're so stuck in a rut you can never climb out. By my calculations you're only thirty-two. There's still time.'

His hands clenched. He turned abruptly and strode around to the other side of the desk, not facing his antagonist again until the solid piece of furniture was between them. His arm came up, a finger stabbing at his former teacher.

'The issue here is not me, Sister,' he said in a voice that sounded as if he was teetering on the edge of explosion. 'I did what you asked. You brought her here. I listened. The voice is not totally bad. But she is not the stuff that stars are made of. And please. . .grant me some judgement in that!'

Kathleen's heart sank. She hadn't realised until this moment that the little nun's courageous faith had nurtured in her a hope that some unbelievable miracle might happen. But of course it was stupid, she chided herself angrily. She could never be the stuff that stars were made of. Morgan Llewellyn didn't know how bitterly right he was about that.

But Sister Cecily was completely undeterred. Her chin came up in overbearing authority. 'We both know that the quality of Kathleen's voice is unique,' was her emphatic proclamation. 'You saw how it left the members of the orchestra mesmerised. You will not find another as good, Morgan. Please. . .grant *me* some judgement in *that*!'

His hand slashed the air in angry frustration and his voice rose several decibels. 'I will not take her on. The voice is classically trained. Much worse is the fact that she has no stage presence. No physical charisma. Nor any natural grace of movement. She walks as stiffly as a robot. Theatre, Sister Cecily, is visual—visual!' he shouted. 'Even opera demands more from its stars than their voices!'

'Then you will not help a great talent?' Sister Cecily fired back at him.

'For God's sake!' he exploded. 'Do I have to insult the girl further in order to make that point clear?'

Kathleen inwardly writhed in her hapless position as onlooker, humiliated by Morgan Llewellyn's assessment of her, and fiercely willing the little nun to desist from making any further appeal on her behalf.

It was as if Sister Cecily had not even heard him. She bore on with her relentless mission. 'Kathleen needs the finest teachers in Europe. . .'

He banged his hands down on the desk and leaned forward, almost frothing at the mouth as he spat out hard unarguable facts. 'You are talking about an investment of probably a quarter of a million pounds! To foster a talent to sing to a small, sophisticated, élitest audience. . .which is actually declining in numbers! Whether you like it or not, whether you refuse to face it or not, this is not that kind of world any more! And I don't want that kind of liability! It's not worth it, Sister!'

His last words were punctuated with such forceful feeling, and with such forceful truth, that Kathleen could not bear any further continuation of the painful discussion.

'You're right,' she said quietly, and pushed herself up from the chair. 'It was only a dream anyway.'

It startled both Morgan Llewellyn and Sister Cecily. They jerked around to look at her. It was as if her presence had been forgotten in the intense battle that had raged between them over her. But there was no sense in it. There never had been. And their argument had only made that clearer.

'I'm sorry that you have been put to so much trouble on my account, Mr Llewellyn. Please don't go on,' she said as calmly as she could, then turned to Sister Cecily. 'I'd really like to leave now.'

'Kathleen. . .' It was an anguished protest. 'I asked you to trust me. To leave this in my hands. . .'

'I'm sorry, Sister,' she said sadly. 'I know you meant well. But sometimes you can't make miracles happen.'

'You don't understand. . .'

It was a cry from the heart that filled Kathleen with sudden uncertainty. She had been thinking of herself, but much of the thrust of Sister Cecily's argument had been directed at Morgan Llewellyn. Had she let the nun down by interrupting?

'On the contrary,' Morgan drawled, his tone loaded with satisfaction. 'Your protégée understands better than you do, Sister. At least *she* has her feet grounded in some reality.'

The nun shook her head. 'Reality is what you make it.' Her eyes reproached Kathleen for her defeatist move before she turned her gaze back to Morgan Llewellyn. 'And you have forgotten how to dream.'

His face tightened into stony pride again. 'Dreams have no substance, Sister.'

She stared back at him for what seemed a long time, and a look of sadness aged her face before Kathleen's eyes. 'I once knew a boy. . .and now all I can do is throw seeds on the wind. . .and pray that they can reach him. This is probably the last time I shall ever see you, Morgan. God bless you, my dear.'

She swung unsteadily towards Kathleen, her hand reaching out blindly. Tears were trickling down the furrowed lines from her eyes. 'Take my arm, Kathleen. The violin case. . .'

Kathleen moved quickly to support her. The little nun's arm was trembling and she hugged it tightly to her side. The violin case lay on a nearby chair and Kathleen bent to pick it up, but a strong hand closed around her wrist just as her fingers touched the handle.

'I'll carry that.'

Kathleen jerked upright, not so much startled by the harsh words but by the electric impact of Morgan Llewellyn's hold on her. Her senses all seemed to spring alive at his closeness. Her eyes flew up to the dark glasses, bewildered and disturbed by a frightening feeling of intense vulnerability. A sharp frown creased the brow above the black frame. He gave an impatient shake of his head, released her wrist, picked up the violin case, and strode over to the door, opening it wide for them to pass through.

Kathleen had to give herself an inward shake to get her own feet and Sister Cecily's both moving. It was perfectly clear that Morgan Llewellyn wanted to see the back of them as fast as possible. It was the embarrassment, she told herself, that made her heart pump so fast that her face was flushing as she stepped past him at the door.

He accompanied them out to the street, a silent brooding figure, emanating a violent turbulence that was intensely disquieting. Nothing was said until they were once again settled in the black Rolls-Royce. Then Morgan leaned down and took Sister Cecily's hand, dark strong fingers enfolding hers.

'You still play brilliantly. . .on the violin,' he said in a gently teasing voice, then, more seriously, 'Keep well, Sister. I like to know you're there, even if I don't see you.'

Kathleen darted a wary glance at Sister Cecily, not knowing what to expect, aware that there had been deep currents running beneath the surface of all that had happened in the last half-hour. The little old nun was biting her lips and shaking her head, uncontrollable tears coursing down her cheeks. She lifted her other hand and covered Morgan's, her fingers stroking over his.

He bowed his head for a moment, then lifted a grimly set face as he looked straight at Kathleen. She couldn't see his eyes yet she felt pinned by his gaze as if it was boring into her with all the turbulent violence she had sensed in him. She stared back, her own insides churning in helpless agitation.

'You'd better be worth it, Kathleen Mavourney!' he

grated, then snatched his hand out from between Sister
Cecily's, and straightened up.

Without craning forward Kathleen could not see his
face and his abrupt withdrawal had left her feeling limp
and more confused than ever. She saw his hands clench
at his sides. His chest rose and fell as if he was fighting
to gather himself under control. Sister Cecily's hands
linked into their prayer position as she looked up at
him.

'I make no promises but this,' he said curtly. 'She
will get the best training for her voice as long as she
stays with me. I'll send the car for her tomorrow
afternoon.'

'Thank you, Morgan,' came the soft, tremulous reply
from Sister Cecily.

'Don't thank me, Sister.' His voice throbbed with
dark conflicting emotions. 'You may be damned for
this day's work. But on your head be it! Not mine!'

He slammed the door on them and strode off into
the theatre.

Sister Cecily settled back in the seat with a sigh that
sounded suspiciously like a sigh of satisfaction.

The chauffeur hummed the engine into life and the
car moved off.

The moment they were out of sight from the theatre,
Sister Cecily dug into her pocket, produced a large
white handkerchief, took off her glasses, mopped the
tears from her cheeks, then began to polish the lenses,
a soft little smile playing on her lips.

There were a thousand turbulent questions running
through Kathleen's mind. First and foremost was the
need for some clarification of why Morgan Llewellyn
had changed his mind about investing in a talent he
had no time for—and what precisely did he mean by
'staying with him'? And, since Sister Cecily seemed to

have regathered her strength and composure, she saw no reason to be tactful about waiting for answers.

'Sister. . .' she began agitatedly.

'It's all right. Everything's all right,' came the calm assurance. She popped her glasses back on and the green eyes shone clear and triumphant as they met Kathleen's. 'Power,' she said contentedly. 'All of life is about power. You have to understand that, my dear, if you are to win what you want.'

CHAPTER TWO

THE turmoil in Kathleen's mind was greater than she had ever experienced—greater than when she had learned that she would never be able to stand for three hours on a stage. Her life was being arranged around her. And yet no one asked if that was what she wanted. She was being pushed out into a void. However well-meant the intentions of the people involved, she should have some say in it. The concept of perfection could be taken too far. Other things could not be totally ignored.

Her mouth set in mutinous lines and her eyes frankly challenged the nun who had been doing a great deal of moving in mysterious ways—with or without God's approval.

'Sister, I'm not sure what you've just won. I'm not even sure I want to be part of it.'

'Nonsense!' The green eyes glowed with the glory of a mission well accomplished. 'It's the future you've dreamed of, Kathleen. You must take it. And I hope Morgan leant something salutary from our meeting today. There are times when he can be extremely wilful. . .'

Her eyes narrowed a fraction, then she shrugged away whatever had given her pause for thought. 'Regardless of whether or not he will acknowledge the truth—and do something about it—the best solution was to bring you both together and let him take care of you.'

This simplistic reasoning was all very fine for Sister

Cecily. The consequences flowing from her solution were a lot more complex for Kathleen. Her mind was awash with uncertainties, and the rest of her was churning at the thought of being 'together' with Morgan Llewellyn. She addressed the nun again with a growing sense of desperation.

'Sister, you heard what he said. And it's true. He can't use me. So how can I accept what he offered? I can't give him anything in return.'

Sister Cecily smiled benevolently and gave Kathleen's hand a reassuring squeeze. 'You are not to be concerned about that, my dear. Morgan will be repaid a hundred-fold. It's all out of our hands now.'

Tingles ran down Kathleen's spine. For several heart-stopping moments Sister Cecily's face wore the blissful look of a visionary. Unfortunately Kathleen was rather short of the pure faith necessary to overlook other visions of the future which did not coincide with the one the little nun had in mind.

She remembered all too vividly that black aura of suppressed violence about Morgan Llewellyn. He had accepted responsibility for the training of her voice only under severe duress. With anger and resentment. And he could very well change his mind on further consideration.

'Sister. . .' Kathleen swallowed hard and forced herself to voice the doubt '. . . Mr Llewellyn doesn't really want me on his hands.'

The green eyes refocused on her with a snap of impatience. 'Of course he does! He wouldn't want you to stay with him if he didn't. And it's the perfect solution. You'll have a proper home and nothing to worry about except tuning your voice into the wonderful instrument it will be. You must tell him I think you should start with Madame Desfarges. She is one of the best *Lieder* teachers in the world.'

Kathleen took a deep breath in an attempt to calm her inner turmoil. She had to fight her way through this mad sense of inevitability with some sane practical reasoning.

'Sister, it's asking a terrible lot,' she protested. 'And I don't understand why he wants me to live with him. It'll cost him even more. And he's sure to find me an irritation.'

He hadn't liked her. He hadn't even liked her voice. Nothing about this whole arrangement made any sense to her.

Sister Cecily stared vacantly into space for several moments before answering, and her tone implied that such practicalities were irrelevant. 'Morgan doesn't even know what to spend his money on any more. Sometimes he needs help. He wasted a great deal of it on an estate in Sussex. All show and ostentation. There are so many rooms in that great house that he probably never goes into most of them. It will be no inconvenience to him to have you live there. And perhaps. . .' A little smile played on her lips and she lifted an airy hand. 'I told him you had no family. Perhaps he remembers how it was for him before he became rich. He was orphaned very young, too.'

The faint smile twisted into irony as she turned back to Kathleen. 'Which is why he took the easy path. As deeply as I deplore it, I can understand it. But, whatever faults he has—and he has many—I've never known him not to keep a promise. Today with the audition. . .and now for your future. Yes. . .' she nodded confidently '. . .he'll keep his word.'

'Why?' Kathleen persisted, still fretting over the

total turnabout Morgan Llewellyn had made. 'Why should he do this for me? I'm nothing to him!'

'You are my pupil, Kathleen. As he was.' A sad look of reminiscence brought a greyish tinge to her skin. 'Such a brilliant boy. He doesn't want to remember, but he does. If there'd been someone with the wealth and will to finance the pursuit of his dream. . .'

She heaved a deep sigh. 'You are what he was, Kathleen. . .a long time ago. . .before he lost his innocence. His pride won't let him admit it, but he remembers how he felt then, and he'll give you what no one gave him. One way or another, he'll remove the obstacles in your path.'

Kathleen tried to fit that reasoning into all that had happened with Morgan Llewellyn at the theatre. It did make a certain amount of sense. Perhaps she was worrying needlessly. Sister Cecily knew Morgan Llewellyn. Maybe she was right about everything. And, if she was, it was stupid and self-defeating to let unsubstantiated fears get in the way of taking what he offered.

If her voice proved good enough, maybe there was a chance of some kind of career for her—short recitals— or something! It *was* what she had dreamed of. . .what she most wanted. . .what gave her life meaning.

Events had moved too quickly for her to associate dream with reality. . .the sheer unexpectedness of the chance actually being held out to her, from such an unexpected source. . .and for motives that were too deep-rooted for her to fully understand! Nevertheless, if she didn't seize this one and only opportunity, what other future did she face? Not to accept, not to at least give it a try, was unthinkable.

Excitement surged through her. She tried to repress it, telling herself to stop leaping ahead until she had looked more carefully at what she was leaping into. She needed to know more about her strange and disturbing benefactor, more about the situation she would be facing when she went to live with him.

'Sister, does Mr Llewellyn have a family now? I mean. . .is he married? Are there children?' Perhaps she could help with them, do something in return for her keep.

'No. It's one of his sins that he is not!' Sister Cecily snapped. Her lips thinned in disapproval. 'Nor has he any shame about it. However. . .' She eyed Kathleen sternly. 'You must ignore the way Morgan leads his life. Keep your sights on your own future. Whatever else happens, hold firmly on to that. It's what you were born for, Kathleen. What you must live for. If Morgan persists in handing his soul to the devil, that is no concern of yours. At least in taking you under his wing he will have done one good thing. It might even help to save him.'

Kathleen remembered the dark violence that emanated from Morgan Llewellyn. And how vulnerable he had made her feel when he grasped her wrist. He certainly had a physical magnetism—perhaps charisma was the word—that probably made him very successful in the pursuit and capture of women. There would be many who would not even want to resist him.

But, surely, if he had such a huge house, she could keep out of his way most of the time? And away from whomever his current conquest was. Stay right out of his affairs. And, if things didn't work out as Sister Cecily so confidently expected, she could always leave.

Besides, even if Morgan Llewellyn was completely immoral in his private life, he wouldn't want anything from her. She was safe. He found her unattractve—a robot. He had said straight out that she had no physical charisma. He didn't even like her voice.

Undoubtedly he wouldn't take much notice of her, except to see to her singing lessons. And perhaps the disturbing effect he had had on her today was only a thing of the moment. He was certainly a lot different from any other man she had met, but he could hardly keep her unsettled forever by that sense of barely leashed explosive power. She would get used to him. . .in time. She would have to if she was to achieve her dream.

They arrived back at the convent and Kathleen accompanied Sister Cecily inside. There were a few personal possessions to be picked up from the music wing, and Mother Superior had to be informed of her defection from the teaching staff.

To Kathleen's relief, the formidable head of the convent accepted the situation without question, expressing nothing but pleasure that Kathleen should be so fortunate as to be given this wonderful opportunity to use her voice as God surely meant her to. She took her along to the nuns' common-room and announced the good news, giving all the other sisters a chance to congratulate Kathleen and wish her well.

It was difficult to hold back tears of sentimental sadness as she made her farewells. She had spent so much time in this place, with these kindly nuns. She had felt safe and loved and understood here, particularly by Sister Cecily. And that leave-taking was the hardest.

Her old teacher walked with her to the convent gates. Neither of them spoke until the final moment of parting.

'I'll come and visit you whenever I can, Sister,'

Kathleen burst out, fighting to control the awful lump in her throat.

Sister Cecily took both her hands and smiled sadly. 'No, Kathleen. Write to me when you want to. I'd like to hear from you. But don't come back here, my dear. I've done all I can for you. It's time for you to move on.'

'But, Sister——'

'Arguing again, Kathleen?' She shook her head. 'If there's no way back, you'll fight harder to keep on the course that's now open to you. You must put all your crutches aside. Believe in yourself and don't let me down, my dear. Stay with it.'

Tears filled Kathleen's eyes. This woman, who had been so much to her, who had done so much for her. . . 'Am I not to see you again, Sister?'

The green of her eyes seemed to fade, as if she was looking inwards to other unworldly things, and even her voice had a faintly distant tone as she answered. 'Perhaps. One day. You'll always be in my prayers. . .in my thoughts. We'll always be part of each other. Seeing isn't necessary, Kathleen. You share my spirit. Now go with God, my dear, and may He bless you in everything you do.'

There was no reply left to make. Kathleen leaned down and kissed the nun's cheek with trembling lips. 'Thank you. . .for everything,' she whispered huskily, the swung away before she broke down altogether.

It was difficult enough to keep walking in her emotional state, but knowing that each step took her away from all she had held dear made it immeasurably harder. She tried reciting that she was setting out on the path she had always wanted to take, but it didn't make it any easier. She felt even more alone than she had when her parents had been killed.

But she determined not to fail the faith Sister Cecily had in her. She would do whatever was necessary to accomplish her purpose—to be successful. If she did fail, it would not be through any lack of courage or dedication or sheer hard work on her part. And, no matter what difficulties had to be encompassed in living with Morgan Llewellyn, she would hold fast to the dream that now had a chance to come true. Sister Cecily believed in it. She had to believe in it too.

The boarding-house where she lived was not far from the convent. The room she occupied there was sufficient to her needs but Kathleen had never considered it a home. It was simply a place to stay. The word 'home' had lost any meaning for her the day her parents had died.

The landlady and the other boarders were acquaintances more than friends, pleasant enough people, but of no real consequence in Kathleen's life. While she was quite happy to join them in an occasional drink and meal at the local pub, or take in a movie, the more general interests in pop music or disco dancing or soccer matches were as foreign to her as classical music was to them.

When she announced she would be leaving tomorrow to go and live with a friend, they all wished her well but were not even curious enough to ask any questions. They didn't care. Which Kathleen didn't mind, since any questions they might have asked could have been embarrassing to answer anyway. She did not have many answers, and those she did have she did not care to reveal.

However the arrival of the black Rolls-Royce the next afternoon raised a lively buzz of curiosity. The chauffeur came in to carry out Kathleen's luggage and the boarders became so involved in speculation about

Kathleen's 'friend' that no one actually said goodbye to her.

She felt no emotional wrench in leaving them. In fact, it was a relief when the car pulled away and all her bridges were burned. No going back. Whatever waited for her with Morgan Llewellyn was her new life, and she had to make the most of it.

She nervously smoothed her skirt over her knees. At least she was wearing her best clothes this time. Although she didn't expect to make any better impression on Morgan Llewellyn, she hadn't wanted to look like a charity case to everyone else in his household. If he owned a large estate, there were sure to be other people in his service besides a chauffeur.

Her green suit was reasonably smart, particularly with the Paisley silk blouse. And although of necessity the green shoes were flat-heeled, they were fashionable. Apart from a soft coral lip-gloss, she had not made up her face, deciding that she didn't want to give Morgan Llewellyn the idea that she was trying to look attractive for him. But her own pride insisted she should not look totally unsophisticated either, so she had pinned up her hair in what she considered a fairly elegant chignon on top of her crown. All in all, she felt she had put as good a face on the situation as she could.

She relaxed enough to think it was a fine thing riding in a Rolls-Royce, although it made her feel a little guilty. There was so much poverty in the world that it didn't seem quite right to be luxuriating in such privileged comfort. But she decided Sister Cecily was right about Morgan Llewellyn's money. He might as well spend it on her voice as on anything as unnecessary as a Rolls-Royce.

Excitement surged again as she lapsed into hopeful

dreams. The journey out of London and into the countryside passed all too quickly and Kathleen was jolted into nervous awareness of the outside world when the car turned off the motorway and meandered through a couple of villages. Despite Sister Cecily's description, she was not prepared for the reality of where she was to live, and when the car turned in between huge iron gates and proceeded along a driveway that wound through beautiful parkland her heart began beating overtime in apprehension.

The house they were slowly travelling towards was not just huge, it was a mansion! Kathleen knew very little about architecture, but she was greatly impressed by the classical symmetry of the building with its elegantly columned portico. She could not even begin to imagine what it was like inside, but she had an awful feeling that she was sure to make a fool of herself a hundred times over before she got used to living in such a place.

The Rolls-Royce was brought to a gentle halt at the front steps. Kathleen gathered herself together enough to alight with some composure when the chauffeur opened her door, but her legs felt very weak and shaky as she waited for him to collect her luggage and escort her up the steps.

The front door was opened by a butler. 'Welcome to the Hermitage, Miss Mavourney,' he said with austere and sombre dignity. 'Mr Llewellyn asked me to show you to the drawing-room. He will join you there shortly for afternoon tea.'

'Thank you,' Kathleen all but whispered, overawed by the huge domed hall she found herself in. It was octagonal in shape and there were beautiful sculptures standing on pedestals against the walls. However, she had little time to take it all in. The butler ushered her through a doorway into a room that literally took her breath away.

The furnishings were so rich, so varied and fascinating. . .sofas, armchairs, cabinets, bookcases, occasional tables on which stood beautiful pot-plants and magnificent lamps. And the stunning design of the carpet on the floor was repeated in oval painted panels on the ceiling. On one wall was a marble fireplace topped by a huge gilt-framed mirror, and a whole gallery of paintings hung on the other walls.

Kathleen walked slowly to the centre of the room and stood in dazed wonderment, her head turning up and down and from side to side as she tried to take it all in. She was still standing there when the door burst open to admit a very angry and flamboyant-looking woman.

She wore high-heeled black boots with skin-tight leather pants. A scarlet silk shirt was a brilliant slash of colour underneath a leather jerkin. Her hair was a wild mane of tawny-gold, swept majestically away from a vibrantly beautiful face which was dominated by flashing green eyes.

She slammed the door behind her and stood with arms akimbo, glaring at Kathleen, her expression swiftly shifting from fiery belligerence to incredulous scorn as her glittering gaze swept Kathleen from head to foot and back again.

'How dare he throw me out and replace me with someone like you?' she snarled. Her face reflected horror and outrage. 'It's an insult!'

'I. . . I beg your pardon?' Kathleen choked out, shocked and bewildered by the woman's words and manner.

'You're nothing! Absolutely nothing! Cheap garbage. Filth. Ugly!' The woman seethed, advancing on

Kathleen with sheer hatred on her face. She swung back one arm and slapped Kathleen's cheek with stunning force. 'You think you can take him from me, you ginger-haired wimp. Then think again! In all my life I've never lost a fight over a man. And I don't intend to start now, you little slut!'

Before Kathleen could recover from the unexpected blow, the woman's hands were tearing at her chignon, pulling it apart, fingernails scratching through to her scalp.

Kathleen screamed at her to stop, but the woman seemed crazed, spitting out the filthiest words in her violent fury. In sheer self-defence, Kathleen gave her a push which knocked her off balance for a moment. But she lunged back, grabbed the open neckline of Kathleen's blouse and started to attack her again.

Clearly there was no reasoning with the woman. Kathleen defended herself as best she could, hating the necessity of fighting but left with no choice in the matter. She got in one hard slap, hoping it would bring the woman to her senses, but she earned a vicious push for her pains and went toppling over one of the side-tables to the floor. She landed with a breathtaking thump that left her temporarily paralysed.

She looked up in fear that the other woman might kick her, or throw herself bodily on to her. The reality was vastly different. The girl was hurtling through the air but in the opposite direction. She landed on a sofa with much more force than Kathleen had on the floor, but at least she had cushions to soften her fall.

Kathleen's gaze swept around to find the source of this new development. Morgan Llewellyn stood near her feet, breathing hard, his face contorted with utter rage. He was clothed in black, as he had been yesterday. The dark glasses he wore seemed to make the threatening violence of the man even more formidable.

When he looked at her, his expression changed to frowning concern. He stooped down and was gentleness itself as he gathered her up and set her on her feet. He hugged her to his side in protective support, resting her head upon his chest, his arm curled tightly around her shoulders.

Kathleen was still sobbing for breath, her whole body shaking from reaction to the dreadful indignities she had been forced into. Even if she had wanted to move away from Morgan Llewellyn, she was too weak to do so, and there was something intensely comforting about the warm strength that emanated from his powerful body. She accepted it with mindless relief.

'You two-timing liar!' the other woman screamed at him as she scrambled back on to her feet. 'How can you prefer her to me?'

'I'm not sure that preference has anything to do with it,' he clipped out coldly. 'I told you the reason I wanted you to leave.'

'I don't believe you!' she snapped.

'That's up to you.' A scathing contempt chilled his voice further as he added, 'But I would prefer it if you did not play the hell-hound with my guests.'

'You call me a hell-hound! Me!' she shrieked, pacing the floor and throwing her hands up in theatrical protest. 'Black Morgan! That's what they call you! And you're the hell-hound!' she spat at him. 'You're blacker than the ace of spades. You care for no one but yourself. You're a ruthless, cold-hearted *devil*! More than that——'

'Then you should be pleased to be rid of me, Crystal,' he said with quiet deadliness.

The words hit with an impact that pulled her up short. Her face worked wildly between frustration and despair. 'You need me, Morgan!' she insisted vehemently.

'*Not. . .when. . . I. . .compose,*' he said with very cold and deliberate emphasis. 'Then people are only a distraction. It's why you must leave. I'm going back to work. I told you that last night. I'm telling you again now. I have to be totally free of any personal relationships. I don't want people making any demands on me. I want to do whatever I want to do whenever I wish to.'

He paused a moment to let that sink in, then pointedly added. 'Think of your own future. I'm sure you'd like the chance of starring in my next show. If there is to be one, Crystal, you'll do as I say and leave. Now. You've already created more trouble than I care to tolerate from anyone.'

Each word was like an icy drop in the atmosphere. It didn't completely quench the woman's fire. She glared at Morgan with turbulent frustration, glared at Kathleen with bitter venom, then began pacing again, flinging out her arms in tempestuous gestures as she spat angry words at both of them.

'If that's what you want, what's *she* doing here? You tell me to go, then you bring in another woman right under my nose.' Her voice seethed with outrage. 'Have you no decency, Morgan? You didn't even warn me it was finished!'

'Nothing ever started, Crystal,' he retorted coldly, 'except in your mind. I never pretended to you. I never pretend to anyone about anything. And my patience with you is fast going beyond the point of no return.'

'Why *her*?' the woman exploded, goaded to one last stand. 'What can she give you? What the hell do you want from her that I can't give you? Just look at her!'

she snarled at Kathleen with blistering scorn. 'Throw her out, Morgan, and let me stay.'

His arm tightened fractionally around Kathleen. 'No,' he answered unequivocally. 'You go. She stays. And what she has is a voice, Crystal. A voice that has begun to fascinate me far more than anything I've heard before. So much so that I'm driven to an act of. . .compassion in giving her a home while her voice is trained to its full potential. That's what she's doing here. And that's why she stays.'

Kathleen inwardly cringed. His description of her as a charity case was totally humiliating. However true it was, it seemed to add even more weight to the insults the woman had thrown at her. And Morgan Llewellyn's statement that her voice fascinated him did nothing to appease the hurt. He had only used it as a sop that carried no real meaning.

However, his words did seem to appease some of the woman's wrath. 'Then you're not replacing me with that. . .that frump?'

'I have no intimate relationship with this woman at all,' was the curt reply.

Kathleen closed her eyes, too shamed by the whole ghastly scene to even watch it any more. She felt totally wretched, unwanted, bruised and battered both physically and emotionally. She wished she could crawl into a hole and die. Yet. . .hadn't she determined that she would suffer anything to get what she wanted? And she did have a voice! It might even be one of the best in the world one day. She lifted her head and glared her own pride back at the woman who thought the only important thing was sharing Morgan Llewellyn's bed.

The flashing green eyes narrowed meanly on

Kathleen. 'I'm not sure I believe you, Morgan,' she said testily.

'You are boring me. Very badly, Crystal,' the threat was back in his voice, quiet but sharper than before. 'I have given you the courtesy of explanations that you had no right even to demand of me. Don't try me any further. I asked you to be gone today. Now get your things and go.'

The woman stiffened, still bristling with furious frustration but realising the battle was lost. 'So you can compose? That's why you want me to go?' she persisted, her pride overruling discretion.

'Yes,' Morgan bit out.

'And I'll have the lead in your next production?'

'You'll have as much chance as anyone else. I make no promises. I rarely do. As you well know, Crystal.'

Her chin came up in haughty nonchalance. 'Then I'll leave you to your composing, Morgan. Compose as you've never composed before, and I'll sing it for you as it's never been sung before. It'll be worth it if you come up with another hit.' She flicked Kathleen a contemptuous look. 'And good luck with the voice. You'll need it, since you haven't got anything else.'

And on that note of vicious spite she swung on her heel and stalked out of the room, slamming the door behind her.

CHAPTER THREE

'ARE you all right?' Morgan Llewellyn asked softly.

Kathleen glanced up, still prickling with the humiliation of being labelled as a charity case. She hated the fact that her carefully constructed appearance had been totally disordered. A frump she might be, but the other woman was hideously cruel in the way she had spoken to her and treated her.

Her blue eyes flashed with steely pride. 'Yes. And thank you for coming to my rescue. I'm afraid your. . .your leading lady. . .had the advantage of me.'

Morgan Llewellyn heaved a sigh. Whether it was of exasperation, relief or satisfaction, Kathleen didn't know or care. She was doing her best to distance herself both mentally and emotionally from the distressing scene that had just ended.

'You've just been party to one of Crystal Carlyle's prima donna performances. All the tempestuous fire is what makes her a great actress. Off the stage it's very wearing, as you've just discovered. But don't worry. I'm sure you won't be bothered by her again.'

'That was acting?' Kathleen asked incredulously.

He gave a dry, cynical laugh as he steered her to an armchair and sat her down. 'With Crystal, everything's an act. All directed to achieving her own way.' He stood looking down at her with a brooding intensity that set Kathleen's nerves jumping again. 'Some people—and there are very few of them—can walk on to a stage and electrify an audience. They're intensely vivid. Explosive in action. Crystal Carlyle is one of them.'

And she was not. Kathleen instantly grasped the critical comparison he was making. She keenly felt her own lack of 'star' quality, which he had pointed out so bluntly yesterday. Was stage presence an innate thing, or was it something she could learn, something she could develop along with her voice? The right clothes, and. . .but how could she ever move gracefully, with her legs?

Despair washed through her as Morgan Llewellyn moved away. She watched him pick up her handbag and a number of hairpins from the floor, too involved in her inner misery to even realise what he was doing. Of course he would say whatever he had to say in order to appease Crystal Carlyle. His leading lady was important to him. Kathleen was merely a responsibility he had shouldered. A liability.

And yet he had stood up for her against Crystal.

And taken her into his home with the promise of having her voice trained properly.

Why had he done that when he obviously didn't want anyone bothering him? Unless. . .unless her voice really did fascinate him.

'Do you have a comb in your bag?' he asked, handing it to her and dropping the hairpins on her lap.

She looked up at him questioningly, trying to discern what was truly on his mind. But the dark glasses defeated her.

'It would be best if you can tidy your hair before I ring for afternoon tea,' he prompted, a teasing smile playing on his lips. 'Otherwise the maid will think I couldn't wait to have my way with you.'

'Oh! Yes! Thank you,' Kathleen choked out, flustered by the thought of how messy she must look and instantly dipped into her handbag for the comb she always carried.

'I'm afraid you'll have to learn to live with my *black* reputation,' he drawled as he turned away. 'People will think what they wish to think. It comes with the territory.'

He sprawled himself in the corner of one of the sofas, relaxing as completely as a great cat. Yet there was still an air of vibrancy about him, of something dangerous that could be ignited at any moment. She remembered the threat underlying his words to Crystal Carlyle and thought the woman had to be right about him being a ruthless devil.

'That didn't seem like an act to me, Mr Llewellyn,' she said testingly. 'It seemed to me that Miss Carlyle's feelings were very involved with you.'

One eyebrow lifted in mocking consideration. 'Very strong feelings of ambition and self-interest and pride and possession. Certainly they were involved. Every man Crystal's ever gone after has been one rung higher up the ladder than the last. She has her eye on making a brilliant marriage. Followed by an even more successful divorce. Another colourful advancement in the life and career of Crystal Carlyle.'

His mouth twitched in amusement. 'This should be an education for you in more ways than one, Kathleen Mavourney.'

'I'm sure it will be, Mr Llewellyn,' she agreed drily. She had never lived in a place like this, never had a knock-down fight with a woman, never met people like him and his leading lady. She was getting a very fast education, considering she had only been here for about twenty minutes.

He made no further comment and Kathleen grew

conscious of him staring at her as she finished smooth-
ing the unruly waves of her thick hair into the best
order she could. She was all too aware that it frothed
out like a cloud around her face, but it was pointless
trying to pin it up without a good hard brush to sweep
it into shape. She put the comb and the hairpins in her
handbag and snapped it shut. When she looked up
Morgan Llewellyn was still staring at her with such
fixed attention that it was decidedly unnerving.

'Red is the colour of desire,' he drawled softly.

Kathleen felt her skin prickle with heat, as if he had
physically caressed her with the low throb of intimacy
in those words. 'I beg your pardon?' she said crisply,
trying to fend off their effect on her.

He really smiled at her for the first time—a white,
dazzling flash that was both wicked and knowing—and
it sent a weird shock-wave through Kathleen's heart.
He sprang to his feet, almost making her jump at the
sudden vitality that emanated from him. She was
relieved that he didn't move towards her, but stepped
over to the wall near the marble fireside and pressed a
button. He did not sit down again, but stood regarding
her with a look of musing speculation on his face.

'I am beginning to feel I was badly deceived yesterday, Kathleen Mavourney.'

Her chin lifted. Her cheeks felt as though they were
burning, but there was nothing she could do about
that. 'In what way, Mr Llewellyn?' she asked, wishing
once again she could see the expression in his eyes.

He gave a soft little laugh and strolled towards her.
'Red and black. . .opposing forces. . .that is what we
are. . .thrown together against our own personal inclination. Yet who is to say what might not be created,
or whose purpose is served best? Yours. . .
mine. . .ours. . .'

He propped himself on the armrest of her chair and trailed his fingers through the vibrant waves of her hair. Kathleen sat stock-still, unable to breathe, let alone move. Her mind whirled chaotically at his closeness, at the familiarity he was taking with her person—yet the fear he stirred could not break the mesmerising power of what he was doing and saying.

'You should always wear your hair like this. It's very beautiful. And with the pure contrast of your voice. . .the promise of fire and passion. . .what might we not weave together, with my experience and your potential? It came to me last night—the first glimmer of how it should be. And now, with you here, it should come more easily. . .'

'What?' Kathleen croaked, fear finally worming through the seductive fascination of the man and forcing the word past the constriction of her throat. She swallowed hard. 'What should come more easily?'

He looked down into the vivid blue pools of her eyes, wide and still with taut apprehension. His mouth softened. It brought a teasing sensuality to his lips. 'The music. . .the music for your voice.'

The murmured answer seemed to wind around her, tying her irrevocably to him. Kathleen was torn between belief and disbelief, fear and fascination, the self-protective need to draw away from him and the strange tug of desire that wanted to be even closer.

Every instinct she had was picking up signals that warned her that his black façade covered the pent-up, seething forces of a volcano about to explode. Then, to her utter bewilderment, he broke the electric tension with a harsh little laugh that ended in a fierce hiss. 'Damn the nun! She has a way of showing me things. . .'

To her enormous relief he shifted off the armrest

and walked restlessly back to the sofa, dropping once more into the corner from where he could watch her without moving his head. He hooked his arms over the cushioned upholstery on either side of him, apparently intent on appearing relaxed, but looking more like a panther in semi-repose.

Kathleen stared back at him, struggling desperately for some clarity of mind. Her forehead felt clammy as though she was suffering from a fever and the rest of her was faring no better. A line of thought finally threaded through her confusion and she tentatively raised the question.

'Yesterday you said. . .you didn't seem to think much of my voice.'

He shrugged. 'It's not the type of voice I usually work with. But even then I didn't deny its quality.'

A knock sounded on the door. After a slight pause, a maid entered the room wheeling an elegant tray-mobile. She looked to be in her late teens and was introduced as Alice. The girl was short and rather dumpy, but with a pleasant friendly face. She was clearly nervous of Morgan Llewellyn, but Kathleen was subjected to a covert but intense scrutiny as afternoon tea was served.

It went right over Kathleen's head. She herself was so nervous about Morgan Llewellyn and the 'purpose' he had in mind for her that her whole concentration was required for sorting out what was happening. He had told Crystal Carlyle to leave him because he wanted to compose. And he had certainly implied that he wanted to work on a new show which might be a vehicle for Crystal's talents. Which meant musical comedy. But just now he had more than implied that it was *her* voice he wanted to compose for. And she couldn't do. . .didn't want to do musical comedy. That wasn't why she had come here at all!

It seemed to her that quite a few things needed to be straightened out between them. And she didn't want him touching her again, either! It played havoc with her nervous system, not to mention her stomach and her pulse-rate. She was not going to be his casual plaything whenever he felt like touching something and his other women weren't around to fulfil his desire for that sort of thing. She wished he hadn't made that comment about red being the colour of desire. It was too deliberate and very disturbing.

'Alice, please tell Tibbet that I'll want her here in half an hour to show Miss Mavourney to her room and get her settled in,' Morgan instructed as the maid finished serving.

'Very well, sir,' Alice murmured somewhat breathlessly, and hurried off to do his bidding.

As the door closed behind the maid, Kathleen decided she had to take the bull by the horns without any further delay. She fixed her gaze on his dark glasses and spoke very firmly. After all, it was her future at stake. The dream that had brought her here.

'Sister Cecily said to tell you that Madame Desfarges would be the best teacher for my voice. She teaches *Lieder* singing,' Kathleen added for good measure. She wanted no misunderstanding about what field of music interested her.

'Then Madame Desfarges it will be,' he replied, and sipped at his tea as if Kathleen's announcement was not of any concern to him. 'She'll want to hear you sing before taking you on, but I foresee no problem with that,' he added offhandedly.

Kathleen gulped down some of her own tea, needing

some stimulant to prove she wasn't dreaming. 'You don't mind?' she asked warily.

One eyebrow arched above the black frames. 'Why should I mind? I gave my word that your voice would get the best training in the world. And so it shall. . .' his mouth softened into less severe lines that seemed to express some inner satisfaction '. . .as long as you stay with me.'

Kathleen felt more and more confused. The man was so contradictory. . .a total enigma to her. She took a deep breath and plunged on, desperate to clarify the situation.

'Is there something I can do here in return for your generosity? I'd rather not be a complete drain on your. . .your compassion.'

'Compassion has very little—if anything—to do with my having you here,' he stated bluntly. 'What I tell other people is for their easy consumption. What happens between you and me is no one else's business but ours. And I prefer it to remain that way. So you will repay my generosity by not gossiping. To anyone. Leave all explanations to me.'

'But. . .' Kathleen floundered, still unable to pin anything down to her satisfaction. 'Of course I won't gossip. I don't even understand what there is to gossip about anyway.'

His mouth twitched into an ironic smile. 'You can be quite sure that other people will find something.'

His answer agitated Kathleen into a burst of frustration. 'Please. . . I don't have to stay here. I can go somewhere else.'

Amusement, irony, satisfaction. . .not the slightest trace of them lingered in the look of dark savagery that crossed his face. The tone of his reply was chilling enough to freeze the blood in Kathleen's veins.

'That nun has challenged me in a way that no one else could,' he said with slow, venomous deliberation. 'I need the voice. You stay here where I can hear it. Then we will see if I can at last measure up. You're part of this plot and you shall share it with me. . .the good and the bad!'

However foolhardy it felt to deny what he claimed, Kathleen could not allow his accusation to pass. It took all her courage to face him and calmly state her case. 'I'm not party to any plot, Mr Llewellyn. Until yesterday you were no more than a name to me. I expected nothing from you. But you offered me a chance for something I want very much. A chance that, in the normal course of events, I could never hope to have. And that's why I've come here. Not for any other reason.'

Scepticism curled his lips. 'Do you expect me to believe that?'

'It's the truth,' Kathleen retorted flatly.

He stared at her for a long time while Kathleen churned over what judgement he was making. When he spoke it was with hard stinging mockery. 'Well, let me enlighten you, Kathleen Mavourney. I don't do anything for nothing. You'll get your voice trained as I promised. But when I need you to sing, you'll sing for me.'

It didn't sound unreasonable. Yet Kathleen couldn't help worrying about what demands he intended to make on her voice. How could she serve two masters if one was in conflict with the other?

'Just as a point of common interest,' he drawled, 'did that devious little nun get you to read *Lorna Doone*?'

Kathleen frowned at his rather disrespectful reference to Sister Cecily. Yet she couldn't exactly take exception to it, since yesterday's meeting had smacked of deviousness. 'Sister Cecily did lend the book to me, and yes, I have read it,' she admitted reluctantly, not telling him that it was when she had been in hospital too. That could only be coincidence.

'It figured,' he said drily. 'And I take it you're completely conversant with the story?'

'I remember it quite well,' she acknowledged.

'Of course.'

He lapsed into another brooding silence. But he kept watching her, making it extremely difficult for Kathleen to swallow even a bite of the scone she had picked up in defensive nervousness. Her mind kept whirling around all he had said. And what had been said between him and Sister Cecily yesterday.

Was he thinking of composing a show around the story of *Lorna Doone* after all? Was he thinking of using her, despite all he had said to the contrary yesterday?

What precisely had Sister Cecily meant by 'the perfect solution' when she had planned the moves to bring them together?

'She's a witch,' Morgan Llewellyn said quietly, almost as if he had been following Kathleen's thoughts. His attention was still fixed on her with unwavering intensity. 'But we'll have to do something about the way you move,' he added on a critical note. 'I'll arrange a course of dancing lessons for you.'

The blood drained from Kathleen's face as she comprehended that he really was considering her for something more than her voice. That he was constructing plans that she could never fulfil. That the possibilities he was envisaging could never come to fruition. Never! And the promise he had given. . .for the purpose of pursuing his dream more than hers. . . When he knew the truth. . .

Her hands started to tremble. Her cup and saucer clattered noisily as she put them down on the side-table next to her. No matter how devastating his reaction might be to her personally, he had to be told right now, before he fantasised any further. Even if it meant he would throw her out, he had to know.

She folded her hands tightly in her lap, trying to hide the apprehension which was quivering through her whole body. She lifted her gaze to his and her heart leapt in more agitation when she found him frowning at her. She swallowed convulsively, trying to work some moisture down her tight throat.

'Mr Llewellyn——' she started huskily.

'Morgan,' he corrected with curt impatience.

'I'm sorry. I. . . I can't dance.'

'So? Anyone can be taught. You can be taught. For anyone with an ear for music it is not a difficult achievement,' he said dismissively.

'No. Please understand. I can never dance. I can walk now. I can stand. . .with some discomfort. . .for two hours at most. I can never dance.'

It was as if her words had turned him to stone. His utter stillness was eerie. . .frightening. Not stone, Kathleen thought wildly. An aura of volatile energy shimmered around him. Like a lethal animal poised in the moment before exploding into action.

But he did not spring at her. He spoke. . .his lips barely moving, his tone low. . .flat. . .controlled with such intensity of purpose that the questions he put to her made her feel even worse.

'What is wrong with you? And why never?'

'I was in a train smash. . .four years ago,' she answered shakily. 'My. . .my knees were crushed. They've been reconstructed, but ligaments, muscles were damaged. What the surgeons did. . .was a miracle.' She shook her head in despair. 'They can't do any more.'

He slowly lifted a hand and rubbed it over his brow. 'She knew this,' he said, his voice still low, but with an edge of bitter violence. 'She knew this!'

'Yes,' Kathleen whispered, fear strangling her voice. 'The sisters from the convent looked after me when. . .when I was crippled. Sister Cecily——'

He erupted from the sofa, a black whirlwind of fury and slashing movement. 'Don't mention that woman's name to me!' he thundered at Kathleen. 'Don't ever. . .ever. . .mention that woman's name again while you live under this roof!'

He stalked around the room, punching a clenched fist against the open palm of his other hand. 'She knew what I would do,' he seethed, then sliced a shaking finger at Kathleen. 'I tell you. . .she is worse than Macchiavelli! She manipulated me. She could have told me. How dare she interfere with my life?' His face tightened to a grim malevolence. 'But she is not going to have it all her way! She handed you over to me, and that was a mistake. I'll change what she's done. Any way I can.'

His whole being seemed to glower threateningly at Kathleen as he gripped the back of the sofa and stood there, his face turned directly to hers. Fierce determination sharpened his jawline. His mouth was set in a thin, savage line.

Every nerve in Kathleen's body quivered with the sense of danger. She had not moved a muscle since he had exploded off the sofa, keeping still and quiet while he raged on. But his mind had been occupied by Sister Cecily then. Now his concentration was entirely on her, burning into her in a way that felt uncomfortably sexual. Even as the thought came to her, the directness of his gaze dropped, falling to her breasts. . .her hips. . .her legs. . .

Her tension was so exhausting that when the peremptory knock came on the door and a mature, homely woman entered the room Kathleen's insides just crumpled into jelly.

'Mr Llewellyn?'

The soft enquiry jerked him around to face the woman.

'Do you want me to take charge of Miss Mavourney now?' she asked, completely confident in her position.

'She's all yours, Tibbet.' He looked back at Kathleen, glowering with dark and bitter purpose. 'I'll find a way,' he said, then strode out of the room on a black wave of turbulent movement, leaving behind him a loaded silence.

CHAPTER FOUR

IN ALL truth, Kathleen did move like a robot as she accompanied the woman who had been appointed to show her to her room. Despite the efforts of her escort to point out various items of interest, the architectural wonders of the house glided straight past her and the interior decoration was a meaningless blur. Kathleen turned her head on cue, even managed to make some answering murmurs, but nothing registered in her mind.

She felt sick, both mentally and physically. Her legs ached. Whether it was from the jolt of the fall she had taken, or from nervous stress, didn't really matter. It was a painful business mounting the stairs to the upper floor of the mansion. The kindly chatter of the woman beside her trailed into silence and Kathleen didn't even notice. She paused at the top of the staircase, retaining her clutch on the banister until she felt stabilised enough to walk on.

'Would you like me to take your arm, Miss Mavourney?' the woman asked quietly.

Kathleen caught the concern on her face and quickly looked away in self-conscious embarrassment. 'Is it much further to go, Miss. . .Mrs. . .?'

'Just Tibbet. That's how I'm always addressed in the household. And no, it's not far. Only a couple of doors down the hallway. Mr Llewellyn designated the Blue Room for you.'

'Thank you. I'll be fine,' Kathleen assured her. 'I

sometimes have a problem with my legs on stairs, that's all.'

'I'm sorry; Mr Llewellyn didn't tell me. We could have used the service lift at the end of the hallway.'

Kathleen shook her head. 'It doesn't matter. Please. . .can we go on now?'

The Blue Room was unbelievably palatial, more like a suite than a bedroom, although a huge four-poster bed dominated one end of it. There was also a living-room setting on either side of a fireplace, a small dining table and two chairs, and many other pieces of furniture that Kathleen's bleak gaze simply skated over. She barely noticed that the carpet was a soft pastel blue which was also the predominant colour in the pretty floral pattern for all the chintz furnishings. Under other circumstances, she would have been thrilled to be staying in such a magnificent room, delighting in every facet of it. . .but she could not feel welcome here any more.

'You have a private bathroom through here,' Tibbet said, moving to a door near one side of the bed. She opened it in invitation for Kathleen to follow.

'Yes. Thank you,' Kathleen murmured, unable to gather the strength or inclination to check over the appointments, which were undoubtedly as luxurious as everything else.

The woman frowned and moved back to the foot of the bed where Kathleen's luggage was set along a wide padded stool. 'I'll send a maid up to unpack for you. She will——'

'No!' Kathleen said sharply, then met the other woman's puzzled gaze apologetically. 'Please. . . I'd rather not unpack just yet.'

'As you wish.' She scrutinised Kathleen's pale face and distracted expression, then added, 'Miss

Mavourney, if you'd like to have dinner in your room this evening. . .'

Kathleen shook her head. 'I don't know what Mr Llewellyn's plans are. What he wants. Perhaps. . .' She raised eyes that were agonised with doubts. 'Perhaps you'll let me know?'

'Leave it with me,' Tibbet said sympathetically. 'If there's anything you want, Miss Mavourney, just press the house-button on either of the telephones.'

'Thank you,' Kathleen whispered gratefully.

Once she was left alone, Kathleen made a slow and painful progress across the room to sink on to an armchair which was set near one of the tall windows. It gave her a glorious view of broad meadows sweeping to wooded hill beyond, but it did not lift her spirits or ease her inner torment.

Although she did not doubt that Sister Cecily had done what she had done from the best of intentions, Kathleen could not help but think that the little nun had grievously erred in not revealing all that she could and should have done. Both to her and Morgan Llewellyn.

She could emphathise with Morgan's rage at the manipulation which had driven him on to a course he would not normally have chosen. Kathleen herself felt like a pawn that had been pushed willy-nilly into a game on the off chance that it might prove a winning stroke. But it hadn't been fair play. And as much as it pained her to give up her dreams, her sense of honour demanded that she release Morgan Llewellyn from his promise.

Just wipe it all out. . .go away. . .make another life. She could not stay here. The cost of pursuing her dream was not only money any more, and she could not ignore the pain and frustration she had seen in

Morgan Llewellyn this afternoon. Furious pride had
voiced those last words he had thrown at her. There
was no way to be found that would satisfy him now.
Her voice could only ever be a running sore between
them.

Time slipped by. The telephone by the bed sum-
moned Kathleen from her dark thoughts of a future
she could no longer see. She was informed that Mr
Llewellyn had withdrawn to the music-room and was
not to be disturbed on any account, and dinner would
be served in her room at seven o'clock.

Since she was not to dine with Morgan this evening,
and the probability was that she would not see him at
all until tomorrow, Kathleen unpacked what she would
need for the night, and the clothes she would put on in
the morning.

She did not feel like eating any dinner, but when it
came she tried to do justice to the meal. Everything
was beautifully cooked and prepared, the lamb cutlets
pink and tender, the fresh garden vegetables absolutely
perfect, the chocolate and raspberry mousse delicious.
Kathleen regretted that she had no appetite for any of
it. It was the best meal she had been offered for a long
time and it deserved more appreciation.

No word came from Morgan Llewellyn, and at nine
o'clock Kathleen decided she could safely retire for the
night. She was longing to lie down and sink into
oblivion. The treadmill of her tortured thoughts had
completely exhausted all her resources.

The blue and gold bathroom had every imaginable
facility and she soaked her tired body in a hot tub,
hoping to ease the aching muscles in her legs. When
she finally dragged herself out of the bath she barely
had the strength to towel herself dry and pull on the
long white nightie she had unpacked. The bed provided

blissful comfort and Kathleen was asleep within a few minutes of her head hitting the pillows.

She had no awareness of time passing, no idea how long she slept before her eyes flickered open to the stimulus of light. A bedside lamp was on. She was too drugged with sleep to recollect if she had forgotten to turn it off. She stretched out an arm towards the switch, then stopped. She didn't know how she knew, but she was suddenly electrically aware that she was not alone in this room.

A sigh whispered through the silence, then his voice, low and weary. 'I didn't mean to wake you.'

Kathleen's heart skittered wildly as she turned to look up at him. He was standing on the other side of the bed to the light, his face in shadow. But the glow from the lamp was bright enough for her to see his eyes for the first time, and the impact they lent to his face made her pulse race even faster. Riveting eyes. . .large, dark, thickly fringed with lashes, and glittering with some indefinable emotion. Whatever the hour was, he had not been to bed. He was still dressed in the same clothes he had worn in the afternoon. And still emanating the tension of a tightly coiled explosive force.

'Why are you here?' she whispered, choked by the sense of intimacy his presence evoked, and the knowledge that he had been watching her while she slept.

He shook his head and turned away. He walked over to the window where she had sat earlier, paused there, then walked back again, his whole body taut with purpose, his jawline set in ruthless determination.

'Show me your legs!' he commanded. 'I want to see them. I have to see them. And I'm going to see them.'

Shock rippled through her. She stared up at him,

wondering what manner of man he was to come to her in the middle of the night and demand such a thing.

'Now!' he grated fiercely.

Still Kathleen didn't move. She couldn't.

In a sharp violent action, he grabbed the top of the bedclothes and hurled them to the foot of the bed. The long white nightie still covered Kathleen to her ankles but the sense of having been stripped of all defences was acute, and everything within her shrank from the man who was so brutally violating her privacy.

'Don't look like that!' he breathed harshly. 'I'm not here to rape you. Just show me these legs that won't do what I want of them. I will not accept *never!* There has to be something that can be done about them.'

'No. . .' The tremulous moan of horror rushed from her throat. Her eyes filled with tears of shock and misery. She forced herself to move, scrabbling away from him, her head shaking in a frantic denial of what he was suggesting. 'No more. . . I can't. . .it's no use. . .'

He swore and flung himself across the bed after her, his hands pinning her shoulders to the pillows as he loomed over her, his face a raging conflict of emotions. 'Stop this! listen to me!' he panted, his eyes dark swirls of anguish, boring relentlessly into hers. 'I want to help you, not hurt you!'

'No. . .no. . .'

They were cries from her soul, but he didn't understand. He saw the pain in her eyes and gentled his hold on her, his thumbs lightly stroking her throat as he spoke in a softer voice.

'I'll get the best specialists in the world. Who knows what can be done now? Medical technology. . . skills. . .procedures. . .transplants. . .they're making enormous strides all the time. Wouldn't you like to be free again. . .to run. . .to dance?'

The sheer hopelessness of it all drained through her body, weakening her struggles to a limp trembling quiescence. Only her heart continued its frantic protest at the pressure he was exerting, both with his words and the power of his touch. She closed her eyes to the tortured appeal in his and tried to find the words to answer him.

'I've had the best specialists in the world. It meant. . .so much to me. Everything my parents left me, all the insurance money from the train accident, every penny. . .to pay for anything they thought might restore. . .might help. They did all they could. . .one operation after another, implanting, repairing. . .all the exercises. . .'

She drew in a shuddering breath and turned her face into the pillow. 'Look if you want,' she choked out, no longer caring if he bared her legs. He had already scoured her soul. And if the evidence that was plainly written on her flesh would silence his argument, then it might as well be done once and forever. 'See what you want to see,' she added in dull resignation. 'The scars will tell you better. . .what I've been through. . .to run. . .and dance. . .and make the life I dreamed of possible.'

Whether her words or the flat despair in her voice silenced him, Kathleen didn't know or care. His hands lingered on her shoulders for several moments before they were withdrawn. But he didn't immediately move them to the hem of her nightie. He sat beside her in a stillness that vibrated with uncertainties. . .the dark turbulence of his spirit restrained to the slow inhalation and quiet release of breath.

The light cotton fabric of her nightie had ridden up

her legs in her scramble to evade his purpose, so he did not have to push it much higher. Yet he seemed to hesitate a long time before he gently gathered it in his hands and lifted it above her knees. Kathleen could not repress a little shiver as the cool night air made her doubly aware of what was now exposed to him—the pale circles around her knees, the long incision lines from thigh and calf—but she remained as motionless as she would have done on a doctor's examination table.

He didn't touch her. Nor did he say a word. Yet Kathleen felt his gaze travel over the outlined paths of each operation and it opened up all the memories of hope and pain and the waiting to know if there had been some success, some improvement, some better prognosis. More and more tears welled into her eyes and squeezed through her lashes.

It hadn't all been in vain, she told herself. She wasn't tied to a wheelchair. She could stand. . .and walk. . . And maybe her voice wasn't all that good anyway. She could find other things to do with her life. It wasn't the end of the world. She just had to pull herself together and make another future. She was only twenty-one, with two or three times that many years in front of her. There was no reason to feel she was dying inside. . .everything falling apart, crumbling. . .

A hand touched her face, stroking gently down the wet spill of tears. She jerked her head around and opened her swimming eyes, some remnant of pride demanding that she insist this all meant nothing. She could survive it. She could survive anything.

'I'll leave. . .in the morning. You don't have to. . .to keep your promise. I'll go. . .'

He rolled his head in a jerky, anguished movement, then with a low growl he gathered her up and pulled her across his lap, hugging her to the pulsing heat of his body, roughly stroking her tangled hair as tortured words burst from him, his voice riven with his own despair.

'This is your home, Kathleen. They might call me *Black* Morgan, and God knows I'm black enough, but I'm not so black that I would deny you the dream you've suffered so much for.'

'But you can't want me here now,' she sobbed. 'I'm no use to you. . .'

'What matter? What use am I?'

He hugged her more tightly, binding her to him with forceful strength, yet he rubbed his cheek over her hair with a soothing tenderness that undermined the resolution that Kathleen was trying to keep to.

'Forgive me for my selfishness,' he murmured. Then slowly, ruefully, self-mockingly, words spilled from his lips, dragged from his soul and offered to her in appeasement. 'I've always gone after what I wanted with an obsessiveness that blots out everything else. I build the vision in my mind and it has to be. I won't let anyone stop me or divert me because it's too easy to lose it, to compromise and pervert. . .'

The passion of his convictions crept into his voice as he talked on, and Kathleen listened to the heart of the man, intuitively knowing he was telling her things he never spoke of to anyone else; his struggle to convince backers that he had a commercial product that would be successful, his drive for perfection, his ruthlessness in imposing his will on others. It was a strange blend of confession and self-justification. And eventually there came a time when he fell silent and he simply held her close.

Kathleen felt no inclination to move or speak. Perhaps tomorrow they would be opposing forces again but in this house, on this night, in the mutual pain of accepting what could not be changed, there was an intimacy of communion that transcended all their differences and brought a sense of peace that was all the more precious for its fragility.

She felt at home with him. . .no longer so terribly alone. She realised they shared the same deep-seated yearning to do something with their lives. . .to make their existence mean something. . .to leave their mark, however insignificant it proved to be. Maybe it was because they were both left without family, without the normal supports most people had, thrown into surviving on their own resources. Empathy. . . compassion. . .understanding. . .it didn't matter what it was that bound them together for these few moments in time. All she knew was she needed what he gave her and it felt good.

'I'll work it out,' he said at last. 'Even if I can't have the voice, I'll make the music I want to make, that you need.' His fingers worked gently through her hair to the nape of her neck and spread lightly around her head. 'And you'll stay with me and go on singing. No more talk of leaving. It's settled, Kathleen Mavourney. This is your home.'

He brushed his mouth over her hair and his warm breath wafted through the silky waves with every word he spoke. 'If I don't make it, you will. Or at least you'll have every chance I can give you,' he said with vibrant determination.

His words struck an echo in her mind—'he'll give you what no one gave him'—and Kathleen realised that Sister Cecily had not been wrong about Morgan. The boy she had known still lived on within the man. He might have grown into a hard, ruthless devil, but he was not entirely cold-hearted, and he did remember how it was to dream.

With infinite tenderness he laid Kathleen back down on the pillows and pulled up the bedclothes, tucking them around her as if she were a child to be comforted and cosseted. His face was harshly drawn with pain and fatigue, but there was an anguished caring in the dark eyes as they softly probed hers.

'All right now?'

'Yes,' she whispered.

'You won't run out on me?'

A bittersweet irony curved her lips. 'I can't run.'

He returned her slight smile. 'I was born lucky. This will work out all right, Kathleen Mavourney. You're not to worry about it any more.'

She reached up and touched his cheek, her eyes filled with deep gratitude and a liking that was very close to love at that moment. 'I'll never call you Black Morgan. Never as long as I live.'

She hadn't meant her hand to linger on his cheek, but it did, long enough to feel the contraction of a muscle along his jawline. And his expression changed. She saw a hard, hungry light burn into his eyes just before his gaze dropped to her mouth, and suddenly the atmosphere between them was different, tense and throbbing with an awareness that was intensely physical.

Morgan lifted his hand and almost snatched hers away from him. In the next instant he was off the bed and stalking around to the lamp. He did not even glance at her before flicking off the switch and plunging the room into darkness. She heard him draw a deep breath and slowly expel it.

'Don't dress me in virtue, Kathleen,' he said harshly.

'I've never been virtuous and don't intend to be. Black is closer to the mark.'

And so it ended. . .the sweet peace between them. . .

He left on a dark wave of frightening sexuality. Kathleen huddled under the bedclothes, ashamed of the treacherous excitement that had rippled through her body at the thought of being kissed by him. It was terribly wrong. And she knew she should be relieved that he had gone before everything was completely spoiled. The last thing she could afford to do was to invite that kind of intimacy. It would make their relationship far too complicated, and put at risk the type of friendship that had to be forged if they were to live amicably together.

Yet. . .it had felt so good to be held by him, his hand stroking her hair. She could not help wondering what it might have been like if he had kissed her. Except. . .maybe he wouldn't have stopped at merely kissing her. He probably took full gratification for granted. She had to remember all the women in his life like Crystal Carlyle.

Morgan had certainly done the right thing. And she was grateful to him. More than grateful. And no matter what he said or did, he would never be black to her. She would always love him. . .like a brother.

CHAPTER FIVE

KATHLEEN did not see Morgan again until the morning of her appointment with Madame Desfarges. But she was not left floating in uncertainties. Tibbet took charge of her. Kathleen very quickly discovered that Tibbet took charge of everything. She ran the household with all the competent efficiency of a top executive.

Kathleen was given a tour of the ground floor of the house the first morning, and a run-down on the use of each room. 'Of course, things will be quiet for a while now. Mr Llewellyn doesn't entertain when he's composing, and there'll be no fixed schedule for anything,' Tibbet informed her. 'Just let me know where and when you'd like your meals, Miss Mavourney. You're completely free to do anything you choose.'

The music-room where Morgan worked was off limits, but there was a grand piano and a very sophisticated hi-fi system in the saloon. This room was rich and elegant, decorated in white and gold, and was designated as the usual place for pre-dinner or after-dinner entertainment. But Tibbet insisted that Mr Llewellyn expected Kathleen to use it for her own purposes any time she liked.

The library was stocked with hundreds of books that Kathleen thought she would enjoy reading. She could be taken on a tour of the grounds if she wished. One of the groundsmen would drive her around in a land-vehicle. There were many garden-seats where Kathleen could rest if she wanted to walk outside. And

71

whatever else she wanted would be immediately provided. All she had to do was ask.

Kathleen soon found that Tibbet meant precisely what she said. Her every whim was catered to with a swift indulgence that was embarrassing. A mere idle mention of something brought results Kathleen hadn't even considered. All her needs were looked after with meticulous efficiency. She really could do anything she liked. . .except go into the music-room or disturb Morgan Llewellyn when he didn't want to be disturbed.

It was a strange experience for Kathleen—being waited on hand and foot, treated as a lady of the manor by everyone she met. Sometimes it didn't feel real, as if she was some kind of impostor, or as if, if she blinked, it would all disappear. . .the room she was in, the house, the grounds. . .everything. It was probably very silly of her—this was her home now—but she really needed Morgan's presence to reinforce the fact.

On the third day Tibbet relayed the message that an appointment had been made with Madame Desfarges for the next morning, and that Kathleen was to be ready to leave for London at eight-thirty. Mr Llewellyn would accompany her.

Kathleen received this news with considerable relief and a buoyant feeling of happiness. She had been afraid Morgan was so involved in his own work that he might put off making arrangements for her. And she eagerly looked forward to having his company and getting to know him better.

He was an enigmatic man. Harshly cruel, yet kind. Forthcoming to the point of unnerving bluntness, yet keeping so much reserved that Kathleen couldn't work him out at all. But if he gave her the chance she certainly intended to try. The trip to and from London tomorrow would surely provide openings for more enlightening conversations between them.

Kathleen went through all her music-sheets and practised her singing. At first she was self-conscious for fear of disturbing anyone—particularly Morgan—but, as she became more and more involved with what she was doing, her inhibitions fled. She didn't notice how many of the household staff passed the doorway of the saloon, or found something to do in the adjoining rooms. The need to impress Madame Desfarges with her singing was overwhelming. She had to justify everything that had been done for her, and this was the only way she could do it.

Excitement and anticipation made it difficult for her to get to sleep that night, and she was up early the next morning, anxious to be ready on time. There was no question in her mind over what clothes she would wear. It had to be the green suit. She owned nothing better. But she dithered over her hair, very much in two minds about what to do with it.

She did not want to displease Morgan. He had said she should always wear it loose. On the other hand, she could not forget his comment about red being the colour of desire, nor the different way he had reacted towards her when it had been all splayed out around her face. It would be stupid to invite trouble by trying to look attractive for him.

Playing with fire was not the reason she was here. And she was the one who would end up with her fingers burnt. Morgan had warned her plainly enough that virtue was not one of his strengths. And she wasn't so sure how strong hers would be either, if he ever put her to the test.

Apart from doctors, who didn't really count, she had had very little experience with men. Some of the

hospital interns and a few of the male patients had
flirted with her, more as a fun way to pass the time
than anything serious. But the problem with her legs
had severely limited any normal social life. And most
men were not interested in her singing. Most women
weren't either. It made her turn back in on herself.
The plain truth of the matter was that she had never
met anyone who attracted her in the way Morgan
Llewellyn did.

But she couldn't allow herself to think of him like
that. Better to think of him as a brother who simply
cared about helping her fulfil her dream. And a brother
wouldn't mind how she wore her hair as long as she
looked reasonably presentable. Kathleen wound the
unruly tresses up into a neat chignon and firmly pinned
it in place.

She was downstairs and in the domed hallway by
eight twenty-five. It surprised her to find Phillips, the
butler, stationed at the front door. Since she had been
living in the house, she had gone in and out several
times without the butler's help. She supposed the
formality this morning was for Morgan. Phillips was
such a lofty sort of person that it surprised Kathleen
even further when he unbent enough to address her.

'May I say, Miss Mavourney, on behalf of the whole
staff, that we wish you every success this morning?'

It took Kathleen a moment to recover. Phillips was
actually beaming benevolence at her. And she hadn't
realised everyone knew what was happening. Although
it stood to reason that very little would escape the
staff's notice, when they paid such close attention to
everything.

'Thank you, Phillips,' she said with a warm smile.
Perhaps it was only politeness, but it felt as if the staff
really cared about her and wanted her to know she had

their support. It was a lovely feeling. Almost as if she belonged to a family.

However, the brotherly idea she had settled on for Morgan was instantly shot to pieces when he entered the domed hallway a few moments later. One look at her benefactor and her heart began racing, her entire body suffused with warmth, and she fiercely wished she were much more a woman of the world. Why couldn't she have the attributes of Crystal Carlyle?

Morgan's face looked drawn and tired. His eyes were hidden behind dark glasses, but nothing diminished the dynamic energy he seemed to exude. The unrelieved black of his clothes emphasised the fact that he didn't need colour to make an impact. He had reached her side before Kathleen recollected herself enough to greet him with a shaky, 'Good morning.'

'Nervous?' he asked.

'I'll be all right,' she assured him.

He gave her a fleeting smile of approval, then cast a bemused look at the butler who had opened the door for them. 'Is this a special occasion, Phillips?'

'The staff thought so, sir,' he replied, his dignity totally unruffled.

'And no doubt the staff knows best,' Morgan said drily. 'Thank them for their vote of support, Phillips. I'm sure Miss Mavourney will do us proud this morning.'

He urged Kathleen out to the portico with a slight hand pressure on her back, then took her arm to walk her down the steps, obviously conscious of matching his pace to hers, and making her agonisingly conscious of his intimate knowledge of her disability.

The black Rolls-Royce was waiting for them and the chauffeur was at the passenger door, ready to close them in. Despite the luxurious comfort of the car,

Kathleen found it difficult to relax with Morgan sitting beside her. She was too aware of him, and not only in a physical sense. She kept remembering all the intimate confidences they had shared in her bedroom, and she suspected he was remembering them too. He was no more relaxed than she was. The car moved off and Kathleen felt impelled to break the awkward silence.

'It's very kind of you to take time off from your work to come with me.'

His mouth took on a sardonic curl. 'When you know me better, you'll realise I rarely do anything I don't want to do. It suits me to go with you, Kathleen.'

'Well, I'm glad anyway,' she mumbled in some embarrassment, wishing she hadn't implied he was doing something special for her. Although he was: giving her a home—how many people would have done that?—and arranging for her voice to be trained.

'Are you lonely here?' he asked.

'No. Not at all,' she answered quickly, anxious that he not think she was complaining about anything. 'It's a very beautiful home. And I'm used to my own company,' she added to assure him everything was fine with her.

He nodded and looked away.

Kathleen surreptitiously took a deep breath. The thing to do was be natural and friendly. Show some interest in him and the things that were important to him.

'Is there still something wrong with your eyes?' she asked sympathetically.

He frowned at her.

It flustered Kathleen. 'When you were talking to——' she only just bit back 'Sister Cecily' in time and grew even more flustered as she hurriedly rearranged her words '. . .you spoke about having had an operation on them, and being worried about how much vision you would be left with. . .'

'The operation was a success. The problem I had was fixed. My vision is now exactly what I want,' he replied with flat brevity.

'Then why. . .is there any reason you wear dark glasses most of the time?'

Again his mouth curled sardonically. 'It suits me to do so.'

Kathleen sighed. 'It makes it very difficult to see what you're thinking.'

'Perhaps it's better that way,' he said, very drily.

'Why?' she demanded, trying to reach at the heart of the man and frustrated by his obscurities.

'I doubt you'd like my thoughts, Kathleen. But to satisfy your curiosity, I wear glasses because I still suffer from mild photophobia—which means an over-reaction and sensitivity to light.'

'Will it go away eventually or will you always suffer from it?' she asked, hoping it would be the former.

'It's of no importance,' he said with a touch if impatience, then sliced her an ironic smile. 'The black eye you gave Crystal Carlyle has been far more of a problem.'

Shock dropped Kathleen's mouth open for a moment. 'I gave her a black eye?' she questioned incredulously.

'Her understudy has had to take over until the swelling goes down. Which hasn't exactly improved Crystal's temperament. In fact she has been quite excitable.'

An intense satisfaction welled through Kathleen. Although, of course, she hadn't meant to cause any problems, she could not regret giving that mean-spirited woman a return dose of heartache.

'I was only trying to stop her,' Kathleen excused, unable to inject any apology into her voice.

Morgan regarded her silently for several long, nerve-stretching moments. A guilty flush crept into Kathleen's cheeks. The high colour threw a greater emphasis on the vivid blue of her eyes. Morgan did not look pleased with what he saw. His mouth tightened into a grim line.

'You're wasting me a great deal of time and energy, Kathleen Mavourney,' he said in a low growl, and turned away.

'I didn't mean to black her eye, Morgan,' she quickly protested. 'It was only a slap. Well. . .sort of a hard slap.' When the only response from him was a distinct sharpening of his jawline, she tentatively asked, 'Isn't the understudy any good?'

He released his breath very slowly. 'The understudy is perfectly capable of carrying off Crystal's part. Which is why she is the understudy. That is the least of my problems at the present moment, Kathleen, so don't let it concern you. And now, if you'd be so good as to contain yourself, I'd prefer to concentrate on my own thoughts. I don't in the least feel like any more social chit-chat—if you yourself have had sufficient.'

It was a firm rebuff of any more conversation, and Kathleen just as firmly told herself she had no right to feel hurt. She was burden enough to his generosity. The least she could do was not intrude on his privacy when he didn't want it intruded upon. She sat very still and silent for the rest of the drive in to London, mentally reciting how extremely fortunate she was to be with Morgan at all. And the thought of Crystal Carlyle's perfect beauty being temporarily marred by a black eye was especially soothing.

Madame Desfarges' establishment was quite near

the London College of Music. Morgan accompanied Kathleen inside, still without another word spoken between them. A maid showed them into a very well-equipped music studio where the highly reputed teacher was at work.

Madame Desfarges did not exactly welcome them with open arms, or even with interest. Her manner was distinctly distant, cool and reserved. She was mature and elegant—a woman of indeterminate age, possibly in her fifties. Her face was strong-boned and handsome rather than feminine, although her stylish black dress, and the very fashionable cut of her short iron-grey hair had all the Parisian flair of an extremely cultured woman.

Her wintry grey eyes skated over Kathleen and fixed on Morgan. 'I am not accustomed to being pressed to take on an unknown, Mr Llewellyn. Let it be quite clear between us now, no amount of money will persuade me to train a voice that doesn't interest me.'

'Do as you will, *madame*,' Morgan replied coldly. 'All I suggested to you was that you listen before making any judgement.'

She turned her attention to Kathleen. 'I'm informed that you think you can sing Berlioz's 'L'Absence'. I will hear your attempt to handle the song. Then I will advise you whether it will be worth my time and yours to continue.'

Morgan sat down. Kathleen was told where to stand. Madame Desfarges settled herself at the piano. She gave Kathleen a glare which suggested hatred more than scepticism, then began to play the introduction to the song. Kathleen's stomach felt dreadfully hollow. The woman clearly expected her to make a hopeless hash of *Lieder* singing.

Then Morgan smiled, and somehow it was the trigger

Kathleen needed to give of her best. He believed she could do it, just as Sister Cecily did, and this time she sang straight to him, determined not to let him down when he had obviously argued her case and gone to considerable trouble to get her this audition.

To her own ear, Kathleen thought she sang better than she had ever sung before, but maybe it was simply that she enjoyed having Morgan listen to her. His attention on her didn't once waver, and it was easy to pour her heart into the words.

The last note faded into silence. Madame Desfarges frowned at her in vexed puzzlement. 'I do not believe this. In all my years. . .only Crespin, the great Régine Crespin could. . . Who has been teaching you?'

Kathleen darted an apprehensive look at Morgan, who had forbidden her to mention Sister Cecily's name.

'A nun,' he answered for her. 'A nun who has devoted her whole life to music, *madame*. A nun who is never content with less than perfection,' he added drily.

Madame Desfarges gave an incredulous shake of her head. 'It is most unusual. To get so much from one so young!' She turned a stern gaze on Kathleen. 'But it could be a chance effect. We will see. I'll take you through some scales. I want to hear your full range.'

The testing went on for over an hour, and Kathleen's legs were beginning to ache by the time Madame Desfarges called a halt. 'Your voice has promise,' she said grudgingly. 'I will say no more than that. We do not want you to get a swelled head.' She fixed stern eyes on Kathleen. 'There is much to be learnt. You have heard of Hugo Wolf?'

Kathleen nodded, hope welling in her heart at the interest implied in the question.

'We will see what you can make of Hugo Wolf. Then Mahler and Schubert. We will begin serious work next week. Since my schedule will have to be rearranged to fit you in, I cannot give you all your lesson times right now. However, ten o'clock on Monday will be suitable.'

Kathleen forgot all about the ache in her legs. The joy and triumph in having been accepted as a pupil shone from her eyes. 'Thank you very much, *madame*,' she could only breathe in delight.

The woman's face softened enough to allow a dry smile. 'I shall look forward to starting with you on Monday. You have much to thank your former teacher for. But I. . . I shall take you where the human voice has never been before.'

She turned to Morgan, still holding the air of superiority that had laced her last words to Kathleen. 'You surprise me, Mr Llewellyn. I did not know your interest ran to the truly classical.'

His smile was a twist of irony. 'I may yet surprise everyone, *madame*. The nun who taught Miss Mavourney also taught me. I take it you have no objection to my sitting in on some of the lessons.'

A quick frown passed her brow. 'I will not tolerate any interference. This girl has talent. . .real talent.'

'I merely wish to listen.'

Madame Desfarges finally deignéd to climb down from her lofty perch. 'As long as that is understood. I owe you an apology for my. . .er. . .doubts. You were right to bring her to me.'

Morgan shook his head. 'I can't take credit for choosing you, *madame*.'

'The nun again?'

'She likes to have her own way. As an interpreter of God's will, she has no equal,' he said sardonically.

Madame Desfarges shook her head. 'She must be a very remarkable woman. And teacher. You were lucky. Both of you.'

Morgan's face hardened into stony pride, clearly dismissing his luck on this particular ground, but Kathleen had no quarrel with her new teacher's judgement. She made up her mind to write to Sister Cecily as soon as they got home. She had to tell her all the good news.

Madame Desfarges' farewells were many degrees warmer than her greetings had been. Kathleen floated out to the Rolls-Royce on a wave of exultant happiness. She could not help smiling to herself even though Morgan looked more and more grim-faced as the car moved off.

'Kathleen. . .'

'Yes?'

He glanced sharply at her. There was no way she could hide the dancing excitement in her eyes, any more than she had been able to keep the lilt of elation out of her voice. His face softened and he gave her a half-indulgent, half-mocking smile. 'Pleased with yourself?'

'I'm pleased that Madame Desfarges thought my voice and interpretation was good enough,' she said on a contented sigh.

He nodded, but the smile turned into a grimace of distaste. 'I noticed you were looking uncomfortable towards the end of the session. I think it's best that Madame Desfarges be told about your legs from the outset, Kathleen. There's no point in ducking it.'

Her elation was instantly dimmed by the cloud of her limitations. 'I know,' she said miserably. 'I'll tell her on Monday.'

'Cheer up! She's not going to turn you away. You've got her hooked with your voice.'

Kathleen threw him an anxious glance. 'Do you really think so?'

'I know so,' he said decisively.

His absolute conviction made Kathleen wonder what her voice meant to him. 'Morgan, why do you want to sit in on my lessons?'

He turned away from her. 'I have my reasons.'

'But. . .won't you find all the travelling a waste of time? And the lessons will probably be boring for you.'

'If you have some objection, Kathleen, tell me. But don't tell me what I should think or feel. I consider that my prerogative,' he said tersely.

Confused by this second rebuff when she had only been trying to consider him, Kathleen rushed out the only conciliation she could think of. 'Whatever you want is all right by me, Morgan.'

He turned slowly towards her and the look on his face was a heart-stoping mixture of desire and frustration. The burning glitter of his eyes shone through the dark glasses with a searing intensity that threw her whole body into turbulent confusion.

'I doubt that, Kathleen. I doubt that very much,' he said, his voice low and dark with barely suppressed feeling.

Kathleen clamped her mouth shut, suffering a feverish rush of blood to the head as she realised the implications of the blanket offer she had just made him. Although he shouldn't have taken it that way. He surely knew she hadn't meant that! Did he always think of women in sexual terms? And how could he find her desirable anyway? She even had her hair all unattractively confined.

His mouth compressed into a thin, savage line and

he turned his head away. Kathleen jerked hers right around to stare out of the side-window, although she wondered if the prickly silence was better or worse than confronting Morgan with what he meant. Surely to heaven he couldn't have meant what she thought? She wasn't flamboyantly sexy or beautiful like Crystal Carlyle. What could he want with a frump?

The only reasonable thing she could come up with was that her singing affected him. After all, music was as much his life as it was hers. And why else would he want to come to her lessons to listen? It had to have something to do with her voice. Yet that didn't make much sense either. He knew she couldn't be of use to him.

Kathleen shook her head in confusion. What Morgan Llewellyn truly wanted was completely beyond her. And it was only making her feel all hot and bothered thinking about it. For all her frantic reasoning—and it was a dreadful thing to admit—there was something in her that responded very treacherously to the idea of Morgan's wanting her. And that was a clear inidication that she had better get her mind on to something else entirely. Like her letter to Sister Cecily.

With intense concentration, Kathleen spent the rest of the trip home composing, editing, and recomposing what she would write to the nun who had been such a wonderful friend and teacher to her. All the news she had didn't really come to much—apart from the result of today's audition—because there was an awful lot she had to leave out.

Kathleen smothered a sigh.

Life with Morgan Llewellyn was certainly not easy.

But she didn't want to be anywhere else.

CHAPTER SIX

NO SOONER were they home than Morgan withdrew to the music-room again and Kathleen was left to her own resources. But she didn't feel lonely. Somehow—and she could only conclude that Morgan had talked to someone—the whole staff knew what had happened with Madame Desfarges. . .the first lesson fixed for Monday, her voice compared to one of the greatest sopranos who had ever lived, the famous composers that had been mentioned. It astonished Kathleen that so much interest was taken in her, and she gradually realised that in the minds of the staff she belonged to them.

She overheard one of the gardeners remark to another, 'Our Miss Mavourney will show them a thing or two. I've heard a lot of people sing! Never heard a voice like hers!' Who 'them' referred to, Kathleen didn't know. It was the 'our' that gave her the insight into how she was regarded by everyone at the Hermitage.

Morgan had not only given her a home. He had given her a built-in support system that automatically took pride in her, was protective of her, and took pleasure in serving her. It was a revelation. She had never expected such a thing. It made her feel both uplifted and humbled at the same time. She wasn't at all sure she was worthy of what she was being given. But she couldn't deny how very pleasant it was to be valued, rather than to be considered uninteresting and insignificant.

She felt even more deeply indebted to Morgan Llewellyn, and began to feel ashamed that she knew so little of his work. There was a complete collection of his musical scores on compact discs in the saloon and Kathleen determined to listen to every one of them with proper attention. There had to be something good in his music for so many people to like it so much. Consistent success wasn't built on rubbish.

The accompanying librettos were there also, which made it easier to appreciate the musical effect he had gone after. There was no doubt how clever and stylish he was at expressing the mood or the meaning behind the lyrics. Or maybe it was the other way around. Whatever. . .after listening to four of his works, Kathleen decided that Morgan was a genius in his own right. He really did have something. But precisely what it was eluded her, and it was still not the kind of music that really grabbed her.

She was engrossed in giving full concentration to his fifth work on Sunday evening when Morgan himself put an abrupt end to it. Having not seen him for days, Kathleen was completely taken aback when he strode into the saloon. He switched off the compact disc player with an air of furious resentment.

'What the hell are you playing that for?' he demanded as if she was committing some unforgivable sin.

She literally quivered from the wave of violence that vibrated from him. His thick black hair was all awry. His eyes, undisguised by dark glasses, looked bleary and bloodshot, but flashing fire none the less. His jaw was shiny, as though he had just shaved. The sharp angles of his face looked more aggressive than ever.

Kathleen dazedly wondered what offence she had

given and tried to find an answer which wouldn't anger him further.

'I was interested in what you've composed. I wanted to know. I was finding out,' she explained.

Her answer seemed to agitate him. He made a sharp dismissive gesture. 'Nothing! Shallow, facile, glittering bubbles! No substance! No lasting power! It won't be listened to in twenty years' time, let alone two hundred!'

In a threatening whirl of movement, he pounced on the libretto she held in her hands. He snatched it out of her grasp, hurled it away, then loomed over her, his hands leaning on the armrests, trapping her in the confinement of the chair. 'I will not have you condescending to me, Kathleen Mavourney,' he said with bitter ferocity. 'I don't want you listening to my music.'

She shook her head in frantic denial. 'I wasn't condescending, Morgan.'

His eyes burned into hers, glittering with feverish purpose. 'I can do it. I will do it. And I am doing it!' His face contorted with raging conviction as he burst into impassioned speech. 'There's not a damned thing I don't know about music. I was taught it all and I learnt everything, classical or otherwise! Don't think for one moment that I can't produce something that will knock the purist world on its tail if I want to.'

She stared up at him, nervously biting her lips as her mind suddenly pulsed with understanding. He had used the words Sister Cecily had thrown at him—shallow. . .glittering. . .without substance—and the little nun had accused him of drowning his great talent, taking the easy path. She could see now that the words had eaten into Morgan's soul. For the first time she had a glimmer of insight into the power Sister Cecily had spoken of. Not power in terms of wealth and position. More a moral power, relentlessly tapping at the innermost psyche of the man.

'You want to hear my music!' His expression changed to one of almost malevolent challenge. 'Then I'll play it for you. You can listen. It's not Berlioz or Mahler or Schubert or like anything you've ever heard before. But you'll feel what the power of music can do. My music!'

He hauled her out of the chair, not giving Kathleen any choice in the matter. His hand clamped around her wrist, and without pause or hesitation he pulled her with him to the forbidden music-room. Even if Kathleen had wanted to resist—which she didn't— Morgan was in no mood to be denied.

It was a strange room that she was so unceremoniously thrust into: clearly a workplace with all the musical instruments and equipment and tables strewn with music sheets. But also a room where he could and obviously did live twenty-four hours a day when he chose to. Two black leather chesterfields faced each other across a black marble coffee-table in front of a fireplace. A modern king-size bed occupied one corner of the room and a pile of large decorative cushions lay nearby as though they had been thrown or kicked off the black velvet bedspread. The carpet was midnight-blue, the lighting very subdued; and that was all Kathleen had time to notice before she was stationed by the Steinway grand piano and Morgan himself dismissed the distractions around her.

The volatile energy that emanated from him was more electric than Kathleen had ever felt it before. Her gaze was drawn inexorably to the febrile excitement in his eyes as he seated himself on the piano-stool and his long fingers rippled down the keyboard into a crashing dissonant chord.

'Don't listen with your mind,' he commanded. 'Listen with your being. Let it bite through your body and creep into your soul. Listen to the music of suffering!'

And he began to play, creating a dark, brooding sound that was not a tune or a melody. It jagged and twisted and thundered and set her teeth on edge with brutally atonal passages. It was disturbing, frightening, intensely threatening, and she didn't like it one bit. It made her skin crawl and it was a relief when it came to an end.

She stared helplessly at Morgan, pained that she couldn't in all honesty say that she had found any of that awful music pleasing. She couldn't even hide the revulsion that was still shivering through her. And when his mouth curved into a slow smile of satisfaction and triumph glittered in his eyes, she felt almost sick with panic over her dilemna. How could she tell him the truth. . .yet how could she lie? Morgan himself had said it was kinder to be cruelly blunt than raise false expectations.

'You hate it, don't you?' he said in a tone that suggested he wouldn't be displeased if she said so.

Bewilderment washed over her panic. 'I. . . I can't say I liked it,' she answered, desperately hoping he would understand that it was in his best interests to realise how dreadful that music was.

'If you don't hate it, Kathleen, I've failed. I've failed to create the effect I want,' he said, rising from the stool and moving around the piano to where she stood beside it. His hands cupped her face, denying her any chance of evading the intense probe of his eyes. He spoke in a low, biting tone that cut straight to her heart.

'When you hear that music, you should feel you

want to run away from it, to hide. You should feel
fear, revulsion, horror. . .because it's evil threatening
you, wanting to grab and possess you. . .a black,
obsessive evil that will never rest until you belong to it
body and soul.'

Kathleen's stomach contracted as he voiced precisely
what she had felt. 'Yes,' she whispered, her eyes wildly
searching his as she added, 'But why? Why do you
want to make music like that?' The sense that it was
an expression of himself was frighteningly strong, and
she didn't want him to be like that. He couldn't be
evil. He wouldn't have done what he had for her if he
were evil.'

'Maybe I had to,' he said softly, and his eyes
narrowed to a simmering look that brought a wild flush
to her pale skin. Her pulse quickened to an even more
agitated beat when his hand slid up her cheeks and
raked through the red blaze of loose waves above her
ears. She had not bothered to put her hair up today.
She hadn't expected to see Morgan until it was time to
leave for her lesson tomorrow.

'What you heard, Kathleen, was Carver's theme for
Lorna Doone. Do you remember Carver Doone?'

'Yes.' The word was a strangled cry. Morgan was
winding her hair around his hands and she sensed
instinctively the danger that was winding around her.
He wasn't shutting himself off from her now. He was
deliberately entangling her with his thoughts and feelings and inexorably drawing on hers, wanting. . .wanting something from her that had to do with
that frightening music. She sought some distraction
from the growing tension by rushing out a recitation of
the story that had inspired it.

'Carver. . .' She had to swallow hard to work some
moisture into her mouth. 'Carver Doone was the man

who murdered John Ridd's father. Lorna was forced into being betrothed to him, but she fell in love with John and he helped her escape from Doone Glen. They had just been married and were still at the altar in the church when Carver Doone shot Lorna down. John went after him and killed him.'

'Very good!' Morgan's smile was grim. And his eyes. . .his eyes were burning into hers, boring into her soul. 'Now think of how Carver felt, Kathleen,' he commanded, his voice throbbing with pent-up passion. 'All those years of wanting Lorna but unable to touch her because she was under the protection of his house. A child of the nobility, kidnapped and adopted as a granddaughter by Carver's father, revered as the little queen by the whole clan. . .so desirable. . .and driving him mad because she was untouchable.'

His eyes flared with a savage glitter and he slid his hands out of her hair and began to brush his fingertips over her face. . .her temples, her cheekbones, her jawline, even the outline of her mouth. . .a gentle, mesmerising touch that was totally at odds with the turbulence she sensed in him.

'Untouchable!' he repeated as though mocking what he himself was doing. 'Carver could slake his sexual frustration with any other woman he fancied. He raped and pillaged and murdered without redress. But he couldn't take what he most lusted after, what he most wanted. Not while ever his father lived. He could only watch her. And her innocence was a continual taunt. A goad. A temptation beyond anything he had ever known. And finally. . .finally the old man dies and he has her in his grasp. . .'

Kathleen swallowed convulsively as his fingers trailed down her throat, across her shoulders and closed around her upper arms, digging hard into her soft flesh. Her mind pounded with the realisation that the fiction Morgan was reciting was not all fiction to him. And the temptation he spoke of applied to her. . .in his house. . .under his protection.

His jaw tightened as though he was clenching his teeth and his eyes narrowed to gleaming black slits. He spoke more slowly, each word an exercise in bitterly held control.

'But even then Carver is thwarted. Lorna escapes him. She runs away. And you should run now, Kathleen Mavourney. Because I've got Carver Doone in my head and I can't get him out. I've tried and tried to move on. To do John Ridd. To do Lorna. But there's only Carver. And the only way I can think of to get past him is to take what I shouldn't take. To take what I shouldn't have!'

The enormity of what he was saying utterly paralysed her. She knew she should run as he told her. But somehow she couldn't. The need in him was real. The wanting was real. That terrible, tearing turmoil she had heard in the music was what he felt. And she couldn't bear him to feel like that. He wasn't evil. He wasn't!

His fingers kneaded her arms. 'Don't look like that!' he begged hoarsely. He shut his eyes tight and shook his head in tortured denial. 'Go! Get out of here! Leave me before I do. . .what I don't want to do!'

Her hand lifted instinctively and placed itself over his heart even as her mind whirled in confusion over what was right and what was wrong. 'I. . . I can't leave you like this. When. . .if you need me.'

'Kathleen. . .' It was a ragged breath of despair. He opened pained eyes, caught her hand and started pulling her towards the door. 'It's madness! I'll go to

Crystal. Then it won't matter. I should never have brought you here.'

Kathleen had never felt jealousy in her life. She didn't have time to analyse the revulsion that swept through her. The cry that burst from her lips had no sense or reason behind it. 'No! Please. . .no! Don't go to her, Morgan.' She struggled to stop him from opening the door, throwing herself against it and turning to plead with him. 'It's me you want, isn't it? If that's all you desire then have me. I need you. I want you.'

The words spilled recklessly from her mouth—words she would never have dreamed of speaking a little while ago. But she would do more for him. . .give him more. . .help him more than that woman ever would! Crystal Carlyle didn't care about him. . .only about what he could do for her.

'You don't know what you're saying!' he rasped, his eyes desperately denying the wild offer in hers. 'Don't you think I know you've never been with a man in your life? It's written in your eyes, Kathleen!'

'That doesn't mean I can't want you,' she argued with a passion she hadn't known she possessed. 'Does it make me any less of a woman, Morgan?'

'Kathleen. . .' Sheer agony twisted his face. Then with a tearing groan he reached for her and there was no more argument. No more control either. He hauled her into a crushing embrace and his mouth swept over her hair with explosive passion. 'You haunt me every waking moment, and even in sleep I can't escape you,' he whispered hoarsely. 'Don't stop me now, Kathleen! Don't ever stop me!'

His hand pushed down to the base of her spine, thrusting her lower body into a shocking awareness of what desire meant. The taut power of his arousal was a frightening revelation, and the urgent, aggressive hardness of his whole body sent a nerve-quivering wave of weakness through Kathleen. But she had little time to think about what she had committed herself to. His other hand wound through her hair and tugged her head back and she found out what it was like to be kissed by Morgan Llewellyn.

It was even more shocking than the rampant maleness of his body. He didn't just press his lips to hers. He invaded her mouth with a devouring hunger that set her head spinning with explosive sensations. She didn't even know when her hands slid up to cling around his neck. They were there when he tore his mouth from hers to breathe in, and the quick rise and fall of his chest against her breasts made her aware of how her body had instinctively arched up to his. Then his mouth was plundering hers again with a passionate intensity that plunged her into utter mindlessness. Even if she had wanted to stop him, she couldn't have found the strength to do it. Shock-waves quivered through her nerves, making them ache with a need for some resolution that was completely beyond her control.

He turned her head on to his shoulder. His harsh breathing swept little bursts of warmth through her hair. His hips ground against hers in a wild threshing of sheer animal need. Kathleen's legs gave way under the draining weakness that coursed through them, but as she sagged against him he caught her, swept her completely off her feet and cradled her tightly against his chest.

He carried her down the room, moving with fast, urgent strides. His face wore a taut, driven look of purpose. His eyes were a glittering blaze of obsessed desire. He stood her by the bed and stripped her of all her clothes with a speed that left her breathless and trembling. There was no pausing to look at her and his hands were hurriedly efficient, wanting only to divest her of every last scrap of covering. He hurled aside the bedspread and blankets, picked Kathleen up again and lowered her gently on to black satin sheets and pillows. He lifted her head to free the long tresses of her hair, then stroked them out on the pillow around her face.

His breathing was fast and shallow as he straightened up to stare down at her, his gaze travelling slowly down her body, feasting on the sweet curves of her girlish breasts, the fragile narrowness of her waist, the wide invitation of womanly hips, the pale alabaster quality of her skin, the startling triangle of red-gold curls at the apex of her thighs, even the scarred legs that had stirred his compassion, then back to the glorious halo of rippling waves that threw a stunning focus on the delicate composition of her face.

And all throughout his minute and obsessive examination of her, the sense of total and utterly defenceless vulnerability held Kathleen in an eerie thrall. For the life of her she couldn't move a muscle, even though her insides were churning in upheaval.

A purely primitive satisfaction gleamed in the dark turbulent eyes that finally locked on to hers. 'This is how I imagined you. How I wanted to see you. The colour. . .the texture. . .the image of desire that burns on in the mind long after everything else is gone.'

Then, as if he couldn't contain himself any longer, he threw off his clothes with violent impatience, shocking Kathleen anew with the naked power of his body. He knelt over her for a moment, darkly dominant, then slowly lowered himself, imprinting his maleness on the soft pliancy of her flesh, imprinting the impossibility of any retreat from this intimate knowledge of each other. There was no turning back, no running away, no stopping him.

And somehow that made it easier for Kathleen to accept what was happening, no matter how strange and frightening it was. All she really knew was that Morgan needed her. . .her. . .and no one else could give him what he thought she could. So everything was all right because it was helping him in some way, easing the torment inside him, just as he had eased hers that first night when he had come to her about her legs.

He kissed her differently this time, his lips grazing over hers with a slow sensuality that was intensely seductive, and when he deepened the kiss Kathleen tried to match the exciting eroticism of his intimate invasion with an exploratory effort of her own. But Morgan tore his mouth away and pressed feverish kisses all over her face. He slid down her body and his hands moulded the sensitive softness of her breasts to the passionate possession of her mouth. The sensations that swept through her were so piercingly sweet that Kathleen could not help crying out, and her own hands flew to hold his head there.

But he would not be held. And Kathleen quivered into total helplessness as he moved where he willed, stroking her, kissing her, even caressing the scars on her legs and curling her toes with the incredible sensitivity he aroused. Never in her life had she been stirred to such sensual awareness. . .the satin beneath her, the silky-smooth texture of Morgan's flesh sliding over her own, the prickling roughness of his hair, the musky scent of him, the contraction of muscles, nerves tingling with frantic anticipation and then singing with gratification.

There was no part of her that he did not make his own, and no part that she even wanted to deny him.

The violent pleasure of each new intimacy smashed all inhibitions, and when he had done all he wanted and he poised himself to plunge past the last barrier between them, Kathleen ached to welcome him inside her, to complete what had to be completed. She looked at the driven need that was etched so sharply on his face and, while there was no coherent thought left in her mind, her whole being throbbed to the chord of one simple powerful word: yes. . .yes to anything he wanted, anything he needed. . .anything for him.

And it was the same word that he cried out as he shattered the last bastion of innocence and took her as his own, driving the pain of it into a deep, turbulent pleasure that eddied and flowed with each assertion of possession, fusing into the wild pagan rhythm of mateship wherein possessor was possessed and there was only one entity. . .indissoluble. . .indefinable. . .flesh unto flesh. . .essence mingled with essence.

How long it went on she did not know. . .time had no meaning. There was no meaning beyond the intense inner world that contained only the exquisite sense of their moving in unison, sharing, joining, melding, deepening every nuance of feeling until even the nuances fused into a blissful roll of ecstasy that swept her beyond any conscious knowledge.

And then there was no movement. . .except the thunderous beat of their hearts and the whisper of spent breath, their bodies entwined in limp exhaustion, the fulfilment of total and complete intimacy a cloak that wrapped them in peace and contentment.

Eventually wisps of thought floated through Kathleen's mind: insubstantial, immaterial thoughts that passed by at a distance. Perhaps what Crystal Carlyle had said of her was true. . . She probably was a slut to be lying here with Morgan and savouring every moment of it. The nuns would be shocked at such shameless, wanton behaviour. Only a week ago she couldn't have imagined it of herself. But she couldn't feel it was wrong. No matter what Morgan said or did that might hurt or upset her in the future, this hadn't been wrong.

And she would never be frightened of him again. He might think he had taken her, but she knew he had given something of himself tonight that would always be hers, that no one could ever take away from her. If she never knew another moment's happiness with him, she could always remember this.

Morgan sighed and rolled on to his back, carrying Kathleen with him so that she still lay in the possessive circle of his arms, her head tucked just under his chin. 'Your legs?' he murmured caringly.

'They're fine,' she answered truthfully, feeling only a heavy languor in all her limbs. But it gave her a sweet, warm pleasure to know he had remembered and cared that he might have strained them.

He ran his fingers through her hair and stroked her back with feather-light caresses that made her shiver with sensuous delight. His chest rose and fell beneath her in a long sigh.

'I've never felt such peace. Such contentment,' he murmured.

Kathleen smiled to herself, feeling a deep satisfaction. She had helped him. For a little while at least, the volatile energy that was so much a part of him was subdued, and the violence of feeling that had tortured his soul had been exorcised. She hoped he would be able to move on from Carver Doone now. If she had done that for him, then she had done something worthwhile. She wanted him to make beautiful, uplifting music that would sing through her whole being. . .make her feel the kind of feelings he had made her feel tonight.

'Any regrets, Kathleen?' he asked, and she knew intuitively that he did not want her to have any because he had none.

'No. No regrets at all. Not ever,' she answered truthfully, then wondered if he would think more or less of her for giving herself to him with such reckless abandon. Perhaps all women did. Not that it mattered. The choice had been made and she didn't have any regrets.

The stroking had stopped as he waited for her reply, and when it resumed there was a heavier possessive pleasure to it, and she knew he was pleased that she didn't feel hurt or sorry about doing what he had wanted.

Eventually the cool night air raised goose-bumps on Kathleen's skin and Morgan pulled the bedclothes around them. He smiled into her eyes as she snuggled beside him. 'For all the feverish fantasies of my imagination, the reality of you, Kathleen Mavourney, is something else again.'

She smiled back. 'I'm glad I didn't let you down, Morgan.'

The soft warmth in the brilliant dark eyes was swallowed up by more intent purpose. His hand stroked down her body and curved around her hip. 'You know I won't be able to stay away from you, Kathleen. Not now. Not after tonight.'

The happiness she felt that he wasn't finished with her was almost too great to contain. 'It's all right,' she whispered. 'Whenever you want me, I'll be here for you. And if you don't want me, that's all right too.'

He frowned at her.

'If that's not what you had in mind——' she started anxiously.

'No! It's just that. . .' his mouth curved in whimsical irony '. . .no woman has ever said that to me.' He reached out and pressed a switch that turned the lights out, then dropped a light kiss on her forehead. 'Don't steal away in the night. I want to know this isn't a dream in the morning,' he said softly, cradling her body against his.

It was some considerable time later that a low chuckle signalled that he was still very much awake.

'What's so funny?' she asked.

A wicked sense of satisfaction ran through his voice as he answered. 'If that interfering little nun could see us now, she might think twice before bullying people into doing what she wants.'

Kathleen made no comment. She had a feeling that Sister Cecily would see beyond the physical intimacy that Morgan was thinking about, and she would not be displeased with her bullying at all. Morgan had started work on *Lorna Doone*, and no one could call the music he had composed for Carver Doone shallow or without substance. The seeds that the little nun had thrown on the wind had reached him. And taken root.

While it was certainly doubtful that Sister Cecily would approve of Morgan's method of unblocking his mind, she would definitely want it unblocked so that he could go on developing the great talent the little nun believed so deeply in. The vision of what she wanted for him, and what she wanted for Kathleen, went a long way ahead of the means to get them there.

'All of life is about power' . . .that was what Sister Cecily had told Kathleen. She had to understand that if she was to win what she wanted. Perhaps there was a lot of power in giving. If she gave Morgan what he needed, perhaps he would never stop wanting her. A hopeful little smile lingered on Kathleen's lips as she drifted into sleep.

CHAPTER SEVEN

THE persistent buzzing of a telephone inserted itself into Kathleen's beautiful dream, spoiling the wonderful mood of it. She tried to drive the irritating noise out. It couldn't possibly have any pertinence for her. It didn't fit at all. She smiled contentedly when it stopped. It wasn't until she heard Morgan's voice that her eyes snapped open to the realisation of where she was and why she was there.

'Calm down, Tibbet. Everything's all right. No cause for alarm. Miss Mavourney is right here with me.'

Kathleen jerked around in wide-eyed horror. Morgan smiled at her, his eyes dancing with sheer devilment. He was not the least bit perturbed that the household was aware that she had not slept in her room last night. Nor was he the least bit concerned that the news of where she had slept would be common knowledge around the Hermitage in no time at all.

'We'll breakfast in the conservatory. Tell Cook half an hour. And get a maid to bring down a fresh set of clothes for Miss Mavourney.' He leaned over and pressed a kiss on the end of her nose before swinging away to put the telephone down.

Although she frantically told herself it was inevitable that her new relationship with Morgan could not be kept secret, and that it didn't matter what anyone thought, Kathleen was burning with embarrassment by the time Morgan turned back to her.

His amusement at the flap over her disappearance faded into a still watchful silence. He stroked her hot cheek with feather-light fingers. 'No regrets, Kathleen,' he reminded her quietly. 'That's what you said last night.'

'I don't have any regrets,' she insisted, holding his gaze with determined resolution. 'I was. . .startled. That's all.'

He nodded. 'What we do is our affair. It's no one else's business but ours. And I won't have anyone interfering.'

Kathleen acknowledged that what he said was true, but she still couldn't feel comfortable about it. Not yet, anyway. 'I'll get used to it,' she said.

His gaze roved slowly over the disordered mess of her hair and he heaved a rueful sigh. 'I hope so. But we haven't got time to make love now. We slept too late, Kathleen Mavourney, and you have a lesson to go to. I'll run the shower for you.'

The casual way he got out of bed and strode across the room made Kathleen realise that Morgan had no inhibitions whatsoever about his nakedness, and she no longer felt shocked by it. In fact, she watched him with a kind of curious fascination, never having been exposed to such total masculinity before. He was beautifully built—sleek muscle and firm flesh—power flowing into every movement.

He opened a door, disappeared from her view for a few moments, then reappeared clothed in a black towelling robe and carrying another. Kathleen was still sitting up in bed with the sheet pulled up above her breasts, and Morgan paused in the doorway. Amusement lightened his face and he tossed the robe on to the foot of the bed.

'There's no point in being shy with me, Kathleen. And I'll only give you the first fifteen minutes in the bathroom. So you'd better get moving.'

Since he was clearly not going to bring the robe all the way to her, Kathleen had no option but to go to it. She took a deep breath, threw off the bedclothes, and tried to manage it with dignity, but the way Morgan watched her did not help.

She was miserably conscious of her lack of fluid grace in getting out of bed and standing up, particularly when his gaze drifted down to her legs and his mouth tightened. By the time she reached and grabbed for the robe, she was trembling with self-consciousness and could not bring herself to meet his eyes for fear of seeing some critical reflection of her imperfection. If he had been comparing her to Crystal Carlyle. . .

She didn't see him coming. She was hurriedly drawing the robe around her shoulders when it was snatched out of her hands. She threw him a startled look but instantly flinched away at the grim set of his face. He held the robe out for her to slide her arms into and Kathleen dug her hands through the sleeves, feeling more and more wretched that she couldn't give him the visual pleasure in her movements that he had given her.

He wrapped the loose flaps of the robe around her in a surprisingly tender manner, then, as gently as one would a child, he turned her around and took her in his arms. But as he softly rubbed his cheek over her hair, his embrace slowly tightened, pressing her closer and closer to him.

'You are exquisitely feminine, Kathleen. And don't you ever feel less than that! For any reason!' he said in a low fierce voice. His hands slid up and tilted her head back. The black turbulence in his eyes held too many emotions for her to define, and he gave her no time to consider them. 'Now kiss me, and prove it,' he commanded. 'Prove you will never believe anything else, because nothing else could ever be true.'

Kathleen was so stunned by his vehemence that she simply stared up at him until he bent his head and, with a harsh guttural sigh, brushed her eyelids shut with his lips. He planted soft kisses on them, covered her face with an explosion of kisses, then took such deep and passionate possession of her mouth that any doubts Kathleen had about his possible disaffection were convincingly obliterated.

He still found her desirable. He wanted her. He even cared about her feelings. With a sweet joy lilting through her soul, Kathleen kissed him back, fervently proving her release from any inhibitions at all.

When Morgan reluctantly pulled away he looked down at her with a warm mixture of simmering desire and whimsical indulgence. 'Mind you remember this lesson,' he said, and nodded towards the door he had opened. 'Meanwhile, the shower is still running and the minutes are ticking by.'

She laughed through sheer happiness, and felt so light-headed that her legs seemed to float across the room. A walk-through dressing-room led to the adjoining bathroom which was ultra-modern and masculine in tone with its white and navy-blue tiling and chrome fittings. Even the scent of the soap in the shower was masculine, but she didn't mind it. She didn't mind anything. She felt wonderful. Her whole body tingled with well-being as she once more wrapped the bath-robe around her.

She found a comb on the shelves behind the vanity mirror and tidied her hair, smiling at her reflection as she did so. She didn't know why Morgan was so taken by the colour of her hair, or even why he found her desirable at all, but she was not about to question his reasons. She glowed with pleasure at the recollection of his words—exquisitely feminine—and certainly she did seem to look different this morning. . .more vividly alive. It made her wonder if her new knowledge was written in the sparkling blueness of her eyes, and if everyone would see it. Had other people seen her innocence as Morgan had?

Conscious of the minutes passing, Kathleen shrugged away the inconsequential questions and hurried out of the bathroom. Morgan was at the other end of the room tinkering on the piano, his face rapt in concentration. The clothes that had been discarded last night were gone from the floor and a fresh set of her clothes were laid out on the bed. She dressed very quietly, listening to the phrase of music Morgan was playing over and over with different keys and intonations. He did not look up until she was standing right beside him at the piano.

'Breakfast?' she reminded him.

He shook his head, totally absorbed. 'Soon. Not right now. You go ahead, Kathleen.'

The faraway tone was a clear indication that he had other more important things on his mind than sharing a meal with her. Kathleen left without another word, mindful of what he had told Crystal Carlyle. He didn't want people making demands on him when he was composing. He wanted to do whatever he wanted to do when he wished to.

Which brought her to the other point he had made— that he needed to be free of personal relationships! Was she counted in that, or was she the exception to the rule? The exception, Kathleen decided. After all, last night had not put him off his work this morning. She must have been good for him. And so long as she didn't make demands on his time, and understood his need to be left alone, he would be happy to come to her when he wanted to. He might even share his music with her. . .use her as a sounding-board as he had last night with Carver's theme.

The intense pleasure of that thought eased her disappointment over having to eat breakfast by herself. However, the embarrassment of having to tell the maid that Mr Llewellyn would not be joining her after all made her hurry through the meal. She would soon get over the awkward feeling, she told herself as she went up to her own room to get ready for her lesson with Madame Desfarges.

When a light tap came on her door she raced to answer it, hoping it was Morgan. But it was Tibbet who presented herself and asked if she could come in.

'Yes, of course,' Kathleen replied, flushing as she recalled the telephone conversation which had woken her this morning. 'I'm sorry to have worried you. . .'

'We were simply concerned for your safety, Miss Mavourney,' the older woman said softly. She paused a moment, searching Kathleen's eyes anxiously, then added, 'Is there anything you want? Anything I can do for you?'

Kathleen's flush deepened and she answered jerkily in a desperate attempt to appear unconcerned herself. 'No. Nothing really. I'm going for my lesson with Madame Desfarges. If you would order the car for me. I don't think Mr Llewellyn will be coming with me today. He's. . .he's very busy.'

'The car will be waiting for you,' the older woman assured her. She looked uncertain for a moment, then her face set in resolute lines. 'Miss Mavourney, I know it's not my place to offer unsought advice, and please forgive me if I'm speaking out of turn. But with your background—as I understand it—you may not be experienced in these matters. And, my dear, I think it would be very wise if you see a doctor. For your own protection, you understand. Mistakes can be very traumatic and precautions can so easily be taken.'

Kathleen's heart skipped several beats as she realised the import of Tibbet's words. She hadn't even thought of the possibility of falling pregnant last night. Or this morning. Madness, Morgan had called it, and she had certainly lost all common sense. She managed a shaky smile at Tibbet who had watched the blood drain from Kathleen's face with even deeper concern.

'I didn't think,' Kathleen admitted with a helpless little gesture. 'And I appreciate your thoughtfulness. Can you recommend someone, Tibbet?'

Relief softened the older woman's face. 'Dr Braithwaite in Brighton. I'll make an appointment for you this afternoon.'

Kathleen nodded, inwardly agonised over her own stupid lack of foresight.

'Miss Mavourney. . .' Tibbet hesitated, then in a soft sympathetic tone, 'I'm sure you have a great career ahead of you. I hope your lesson goes well this morning.'

Kathleen met her eyes in grateful understanding. Live your own life, she was saying. Morgan's desire for any woman had never been enduring. Even Sister Cecily had advised her that how Morgan lived his life had to be no concern of hers. She had to keep her sights set on her own future no matter what else happened.

'I'll try my best, Tibbet,' she said, forced to get her feet firmly replanted on sensible ground. 'And please, if ever you think I need advice, don't hesitate to give it.'

'Whenever I can be of some help to you, I'll do the best I can.'

The warm reply put Kathleen more at ease with the

situation she found herself in. Tibbet cared about her. Not only that, she had given a clear indication that she regarded Kathleen as a worthwhile person in her own right, and would be respected as such no matter what her relationship was with Morgan. Which was their business and no one else's.

Tibbet had turned away and was moving towards the door when another thought struck Kathleen. 'Why are you so kind to me?' she asked impulsively. 'I mean. . .it's so good of you. . .and I can't thank you enough for. . .'

'Part of the service, Miss Mavourney,' Tibbet replied matter-of-factly, but a slight, musing little smile softened her mouth as she reached for the doorknob.

'I feel it's more than that,' Kathleen pressed.

The woman paused, and for a moment there was a look on her face. . .a sense of mission. . .or a need for order and perfection. . .impossible to define exactly, and probably it was integral to an air of unshakeable authority. Nevertheless, Tibbet's next words were more discomfiting than reassuring.

'I met your nun—Mr Llewellyn's old teacher—the day she came here. I showed her through the Hermitage.'

Kathleen flushed in acute embarrassment. 'Did Sister Cecily ask you to. . .to look out for me?'

Tibbet shook her head. 'Your name wasn't even mentioned, Miss Mavourney.'

'Then. . . I don't understand. . .'

That same enigmatic little smile flitted over her mouth again. 'A most interesting woman. We simply had a mutual understanding of what's important. And what's not. I'll let you know the time of your appointment when you return from your lesson.'

It was a judgement which prompted Kathleen to

spend the trip into London reaffirming her own goals. Whatever she shared with Morgan was a side issue. Just as he didn't let anything interfere with his composing, she must not let anything interfere with her singing. All the same, she couldn't help hoping that the intimacy they had shared last night would continue for a long time. What she would like best would be sharing everything with him. But that was probably hoping for too much.

Madame Desfarges was clearly pleased that Morgan had not accompanied Kathleen to the lesson. 'We have much to do. He would only be a distraction. And we must have full concentration,' she said sternly. 'Now we will begin——'

'Madame Desfarges, there is something I have to tell you first,' Kathleen interrupted, hating the necessity, but grimly resolved on revealing the problem which would bar her from any normal career.

The formidable Frenchwoman sat frowning in silence for several minutes after Kathleen had explained about her legs, then shrugged the problem aside as if it was of no concern. 'When the time comes, we will see what can be arranged. First the work. If there is no voice, then it does not matter whether you have legs or not.'

When it came to being a task-mistress and a perfectionist, Kathleen soon discovered that Madame Desfarges was a martinet in a class of her own. Scales had to be even, rapid and perfectly distinct. Exercises in breath control were mandatory for the difficult runs in Handel and Mozart. She had to produce a beautifully smooth line, a focused tone, plus a command and generosity of emotion in interpretation. And that was only the beginning.

At the end of the lesson Madame Desfarges handed

her a schedule. 'There are the times you are to come to me. I have arranged for you to go from here to a teacher in foreign languages twice a week. Monsieur Lemesurier will coach you in French, German and Italian. Accents must be precise if you are to sing the great composers with authority. Later we will probably add Spanish and Russian.'

Kathleen frowned over the extra expense the language lessons would incur. 'I'll have to ask Mr Llewellyn if it's all right with him, *madame*.'

A haughty arrogance flitted over her face. 'My dear girl, Mr Llewellyn would not have brought you to me if he had half-measures in mind. Consult him by all means, but this is the regimen you will follow.'

Kathleen wanted to consult Morgan, but it turned out to be a more difficult proposition than she had foreseen. When she arrived back at the Hermitage she discovered from Phillips, the butler, that Morgan had not emerged from the music-room all morning.

'I have to see him,' she muttered, more to herself than Phillips.

The butler cleared his throat and lowered his eyebrows in something approaching a conspiratorial manner. 'If you don't mind my saying so, Miss Mavourney, it would not be wise to go to the music-room uninvited. Mr Llewellyn can be extremely *tetchy* if he is interrupted when he doesn't wish to be. Much better to wait until he. . .er. . .comes out of the creative process.'

It was well-meant advice and Kathleen took it. Her disappointment at Morgan's inaccessibility was slightly eased by the realisation that Phillips, as well as Tibbet, was intent on protecting her from making mistakes. She ruefully wondered if everyone at the Hermitage thought she was a babe who had got well and truly lost in the woods with Morgan Llewellyn, but she was grateful for the guidance offered.

She ate lunch alone, then went into Brighton to keep the appointment Tibbet had made for her. Dr Braithwaite treated the whole thing in a smooth, efficient, matter-of-fact manner. Kathleen was not made to feel an absolute idiot, and by the time she left his clinic she was at last well-informed and well-equipped to look after herself. However, she had to work hard at pushing aside the sense of being wantonly immoral for actually planning to sleep with Morgan whenever he wanted her to.

Nevertheless, despite everything she'd been taught throughout her convent education, it didn't feel like a sin. And if it was, she was prepared to pay for it. Her life had been so barren of personal involvement up until now. She might never meet another man who affected her as deeply as Morgan did. Maybe she would never experience the same feelings with anyone else. Right or wrong, she was determined to go on with it. As long as it lasted.

The afternoon had turned grey and was drizzling with rain. When she arrived home, Phillips came hurrying out to the car with a huge black umbrella, ready to protect her from every inclement force of nature.

'Is Mr Llewellyn still in the music-room?' Kathleen asked anxiously as they walked up the front steps.

'No, Miss. He's gone out riding.'

'In the rain?'

A pained look crossed Phillips' face. 'I doubt Mr Llewellyn would notice the rain, Miss Mavourney. Not in his. . .er. . .present mood.'

Kathleen sighed. 'A bit tetchy, Phillips?'

'Yes, Miss. I would say. . .very. . .tetchy.'

Kathleen wanted to ask if Morgan had enquired after her whereabouts, but on second thoughts she was sure Phillips would tell her if that was so, and she didn't want to sound as if she felt neglected. She had chosen to stay with Morgan last night. That didn't give her the right to expect any attention from him today. But she needed—and very much wanted—to see him.

And she did. . .from the tall windows in the Blue Room. . .a rider in black on a black horse, galloping hell for leather across the meadows and leaping every hedge in sight. No one else but Morgan would be out in this weather expending so much violent energy. The peace he had found with her certainly hadn't lasted long. He looked as if he was being driven by the same demons of frustration that had been unleashed last night.

In the hope that he might seek her company when he came in from his ride, Kathleen went down to the saloon. Madame Desfarges had lent her some music tapes which Kathleen was to listen to, so she played them over and over. But Morgan did not appear. Not before dinner, not during dinner, nor after dinner. Kathleen reasoned that he must be working on a new idea.

However, she found it was one thing to reason with her mind, quite another to keep her emotions under control. She felt miserably bereft as she went upstairs and got ready for bed. She even started to wonder if going to the doctor had been a waste of time. Perhaps Morgan didn't need her any more. She had served his purpose last night and that was that.

But it wasn't what he had said. He had said he wouldn't be able to leave her alone.

Kathleen hoped he had spoken the truth.

She switched off her light and settled herself to

sleep. The memory of Sister Cecily saying that Morgan was shameless flitted through her mind. She felt a bit guilty over being shameless herself, but that didn't stop her wanting to have him with her, even if it was only to relieve his frustration.

The whisper of her name and the gentle stroking of her hair away from her temples drew her out of sleep. Pleasure rippled through her even before she opened her eyes and saw his dark form leaning over her. Her arms lifted instinctively to encircle his neck and hold him there. He had come to her! She wanted him to stay. . .to hold her, to make love to her, to share himself with her.

He kissed her with a hard, devouring hunger that seemed to say that he had missed her as much as she had missed him, and, even though Kathleen knew that couldn't be true, she didn't care. All the pent-up fears and doubts and embarrassments of the long day made the passion of his kiss all the sweeter and her own response all the more fervent.

He didn't ask. . .she didn't answer. . .not a word was spoken. Morgan tore himself out of her embrace and wrenched off the robe he wore. Kathleen lifted the bedclothes for him. He came to her, his strong naked body spreading a different warmth over hers. Slowly he gathered up her nightie and pulled it over her head, leaving her arms extended in the sleeves long enough for him to take her uplifted breasts in his mouth. Exquisite pleasure. She fought her way out of the constricting gown, desperate to hold him to her. A thrill of exultation powered through her when he cried out at the possessive rake of her hands over the tightly bunched muscles of his back. His breath came in harsh gasps as he dragged her nearer to him and thrust hard against her body.

She arched in convulsive reaction as he entered her. His arms cradled her hips and rolled her around him, sensitising every nerve within her to an incredible pitch of almost unbearable excitement. Her whole body clenched in pounding anticipation, then seemed to explode into melting limpness. He began a fierce, relentless rhythm of savage possession, taking her to the crest of one wave after another of endlessly rolling pleasure.

There was a wild insatiability about Morgan's need for her, a demanding domination that would not be content until she gave him all he wanted: the absolute triumph of knowing she moved only to his will, that he was the master of both his fate and hers. And that, without her, he was nothing. When at last he allowed himself to climax, he wound his arms around her and kept her pinned to him with obsessive possessiveness.

Still he said nothing. Kathleen was beyond moving, let alone thinking or speaking. She lay a willing prisoner in his embrace, secure and warm against the hard pulsing heat and strength of his flesh. She didn't remember who she was. She didn't remember anything. The only reality was his and her hearts beating in unison. Together.

CHAPTER EIGHT

WHEN Kathleen woke the next morning Morgan was gone from her bed. She did not know if he had stayed and slept with her and simply risen early, or had slipped away from her soon after she had fallen asleep. This last was a disturbing thought. It suggested he was only using her as some kind of escape-valve for his pent-up frustrations. Kathleen didn't want to believe that, or even think that it could be true. But it was still weighing on her mind when Alice, the maid, knocked and came in with the early morning cup of tea.

'Mr Llewellyn said to tell you he would be accompanying you to your lesson this morning, Miss Mavourney,' Alice announced, instantly lifting Kathleen's gloom.

'Does he know what time we have to leave?' she asked, remembering that there had been no opportunity to show him Madame Desfarges' schedule.

'Yes, Miss Mavourney. Tibbet informed him from the list you gave her yesterday.'

Kathleen relaxed, delighted that Morgan was going to spend time with her today. The maid was on the point of leaving the room when an unwelcome doubt forced another question. 'Alice, is Mr Llewellyn in the music-room?'

'Yes, Miss.'

Kathleen waved the maid on and tried to resign herself to the probability that Morgan might become so immersed in his work again that she would not see him after all. But at least he had thought of her. She wasn't only a sexual convenience to be used during the night.

Kathleen did her best to repress the buoyant anticipation that kept bubbling up as she bathed and dressed. The conflict between excitement and hard common sense made it difficult for her to enjoy breakfast. However, by the time she was ready to leave for her lesson she had almost quelled any expectation of Morgan's joining her for the trip into London.

When she found him actually waiting for her in the domed hallway, all her enforced restraints were instantly shattered by a burst of joy. Her heart danced, her blue eyes sparkled with happiness, and it was all she could do not to fling her arms around his neck when he smiled at her.

But the warm pleasure that had flashed across his face faded into a self-mocking irony as he touched her cheek in an indulgent salute. 'There are moments when I wish you weren't quite so transparent in your feelings, Kathleen Mavourney.'

'I'm just glad you're coming with me,' she said quickly, sensing that he didn't want to feel obliged to respond to her needs. 'Madame Desfarges has organised foreign language lessons for me and I didn't get the chance to ask you about them yesterday.'

His mouth pulled down into a savage grimace. 'Yesterday I was trying to force something that can't be forced. The Little Scourge of my Life hit the nail on the head when she said I've had things come too easily for far too long. Whether I like it or not, I've got to learn patience if I'm to get what I'm going after.'

He tucked her arm around his to take her out to the car and Kathleen couldn't resist hugging close to him. It brought a whimsical smile to his lips and she felt wonderfully light-hearted—even light-footed—as they walked down the steps together. Once they were settled in the Rolls, Morgan turned to her, a soft, relaxed expression on his usually hard face.

'So what's all this about language lessons?' he asked.

Kathleen explained to him at great length, so delighted to have his attention that she told him all about yesterday's session with Madame Desfarges. Morgan seemed to find it interesting, nodding encouragement, asking questions, telling her the language lessons were fine by him.

His manner was so approachable that Kathleen decided this was the perfect opportunity to find out more about him. Now that she knew what Morgan was working on, she was curious about how he planned to adapt the story of *Lorna Doone* to musical theatre. She put a few tentative questions, wary of his response, and was surprised and delighted with his forthright replies.

She learnt a new appreciation of his talent as he replotted the book into scenes he would use, outlining the dramatic potential of each and every one of them. . .how they would link together and keep building emotional tension towards the climactic wedding scene in the church.

Kathleen would have liked the conversation to go on much longer but it was necessarily terminated by their arrival at their destination. Madame Desfarges glared disapprovingly at Morgan when he turned up at the lesson with Kathleen, but he sat silently throughout, giving the woman no reason to complain about his presence.

On the way home he did not invite conversation, and Kathleen recognised the rapt look of concentration on his face and remained silent. Occasionally she heard him humming and his fingers tapped measured patterns across his knee. When they arrived back at the Hermitage he left her without a word and disappeared into the music-room.

But he did not stay there for the rest of the day. Nor did he emerge in a black mood. They had dinner together, and Kathleen enjoyed the heady pleasure of sharing opinions about the great composers and singers with someone who knew precisely what she was talking about. And that night Morgan made love to her with a slow sensuality that taught her other ecstatic pleasures.

The week that followed was sheer heaven to Kathleen. Morgan gave up his composing entirely and devoted practically every minute to her. In fact his concentration on her had an intensity that suggested that he wanted or needed to immerse himself in her, absorbing everything there was to know about her.

Kathleen was only too willing to oblige him, joyously relating various facets of her life, her thoughts and feelings on all manner of subjects. . .except Morgan himself. Those thoughts and feelings she kept to herself, wary that he might interpret them as a claim on him, or even a demand that he should return her love. Their relationship was so new, so precious to her, that anything that might threaten it was total anathema to her.

Yet there were moments when Morgan surprised and thrilled her with unexpected gestures. He took her on a picnic, choosing a beautiful spot by the stream that ran through the meadows on his estate. Bluebells were growing under the trees. He picked a small bunch and brought it to her, playfully stroking the soft blooms over her cheeks.

'Not quite the colour of your eyes, but close,' he said, and his smile seemed warm and tenderly loving as he softly added, 'The windows of your soul. Through those lovely shining eyes you show me another world, Kathleen. One that I didn't believe existed. But it does. I can feel it now. . .with you.'

Kathleen didn't know what to say. She didn't quite know what he meant. 'Is it good?' she asked, hoping it was a world he wanted.

He laughed with open pleasure, and there was not the slightest hint of cynicism in his eyes when he answered, 'Yes. It's good. Better than you could ever imagine, Kathleen.'

He laid the bluebells on her lap and picked up her hand, turning it around in his as if assessing it for some special quality. 'So small and delicate,' he murmured. 'Yet its touch is like a blessing. A blessing I'm not worthy of. But as long as you give it, I'll take it.'

His eyes lifted to hers again, a swirl of dark turbulence overriding the gentleness of his manner. 'I have to. It's probably the only chance I'll ever have. You understand that, don't you, Kathleen?'

'Yes,' she said, although she didn't understand. She only sensed his need for her to agree with him, and his need to take whatever it was she gave him.

Afterwards she wondered if this had been Morgan's oblique way of asking her forbearance, perhaps even forgiveness for what was to follow. The day after their picnic he went back to work. His total absorption in her was over. The need to compose obsessed him once again.

However, one thing had changed. The music-room was no longer forbidden to her. Kathleen recognised this as an enormous concession. She was being given something she had never expected, something so marvellous to her that she was not about to do anything that might disturb Morgan's concentration or alienate him in any way. She hoarded every moment of their time together in her memory, never certain of when she would see him again and always conscious that she mustn't make demands. And she was infinitely rewarded for her patience and understanding of his needs.

He did not accompany her to London on the days she had foreign language tuition, but he almost invariably invited her into the music-room as soon as she arrived home. Sometimes he asked her to sing what Madame Desfarges had been teaching her. Other times he simply wanted her to be there with him as he worked on his compositions.

Kathleen found it fascinating to listen to him developing a musical theme. When he was working she was careful never to speak to him unless he spoke to her, but he would frequently look up from the piano and study her in an abstracted way.

As the days passed into weeks, Morgan's musical score for *Lorna Doone* grew into an impressive number of themes and songs. Kathleen loved the music he wrote for John Ridd. It expressed a wonder and delight in Lorna's beauty, and his love was overlaid with a tenderness that was intensely moving. It was Kathleen's favourite daydream that Morgan was pouring what he felt for her into John Ridd's songs, but he never intimated that this was so, and of course she didn't dare ask him. She grew impatient to hear what he would compose for Lorna, but he never discussed it with her, nor played anything that Kathleen could identify as in character for the central star of his show.

There were no visitors to the Hermitage during this time, and Kathleen's only outside contacts were her teachers. The life she and Morgan led was extremely narrow, revolving entirely around his music, her singing, and the physical intimacy they shared at night.

However much she tried to deny the thought that what they shared was only an interlude for him—an interlude that would finish once he had achieved the goal he had set himself—Kathleen could not entirely push it from her mind.

She knew instinctively that she was tied in with his obsession to show the world—and Sister Cecily—that his genius extended a long way beyond what he had previously done. She wasn't quite sure what role she fulfilled throughout this creative process, but she was very much afraid that her present place in his life would be vastly diminished when he had succeeded in composing what he wanted.

When he re-entered his celebrity world to set the wheels in motion for launching *Lorna Doone*. . .would he still want her then? Would he need her any more? It could very well be that, when it came to staging the show he had created with her, he would turn back to Crystal Carlyle, who could help him sell it to the public.

It was a possibility that Kathleen could not ignore, and she tried to arm herself against it by concentrating hard on her own career, determinedly carrying through on everything Madame Desfarges set for her to do. She had to learn to be independent, even though Morgan was sometimes impatient with her dedication.

The time would almost certainly come when she had to be independent, and Kathleen recognised that. No meaningful relationship could be obtained by one person giving everything and the other person taking everything. There had to be a mutuality in sharing.

One afternoon when she was in the saloon listening to a tape, from which she had to absorb a singing technique, Morgan came to the doorway. Without any by-your-leave or the slightest consideration for what she was doing he demanded that she switch off the tape and come with him. Kathleen quietly but stubbornly took a stand.

'Morgan, I don't interrupt you when you're working.'

'You can listen to that any time,' he argued. 'I want you to come and hear——'

'I have wants and needs too,' she cut in, suddenly feeling that he only ever considered himself, and she didn't think that was being totally fair.

'This is more important,' he said tersely.

'For you it is. For me, this is more important. This is my life's work.' Her chin lifted defiantly as she added, 'I don't make demands on you, Morgan. I never have——'

'Nor you damned well should!' he retorted, his face darkening with anger. 'Perhaps the fact that I pay for your needs has slipped your mind. Or are you like every other woman, who thinks if she shares a man's bed it's repayment enough?'

The acid sting of his words whipped all colour from her cheeks and she stared at him in stricken pain. 'Is that how you think of it, Morgan? That you're paying. . .so you have the right to take all you want of me?'

A violent wash of emotion raged across his face. Whether it was desire or despair or simply furious impatience with her Kathleen could not tell. It made her wish she had not spoken at all. Everything within her shrank from the idea that he thought he had bought her body and soul. She didn't even want to know if it was true, because she didn't know how she would bear it if it was.

He spoke with bitter pride. 'Tell me what I've taken from you that you didn't want to give, Kathleen. I seem to have deluded myself about you. I thought you liked giving. . .what you gave.'

Kathleen had the dreadful sense of their relationship shattering into irretrievable pieces. But she had to stay true to her own ideas and ideals. She could not allow Morgan to completely dominate her life.

'I'm sorry if I offend you, Morgan. But I have my own dream to pursue, my own life to consider. . .the goals I want to reach, what I must achieve. And I also need to be my own person,' she said in quiet desperation. 'But I didn't mean to suggest that I was not willing or happy to. . .to have what we share together.'

'But now you think you have enough power over me to lay down your own terms. Is that it?' he mocked savagely.

'No! I don't think that!' she cried, panic welling through her in a sickening surge. She was only asking him to treat her reasonably. Was that so wrong?

'Good!' he snapped. A cold ruthlessness bit into every word as he added, 'And to make it perfectly clear—in case you have been entertaining delusions—the terms of our relationship are precisely what I stated on the day you arrived. You'll get whatever training your voice requires, but when I need you to sing, you'll sing for me. And that happens to be now! Not when you feel like deigning to oblige me. Now!'

His words chilled her to the bone, freezing the weakening churn of emotions his displeasure had stirred. She would not. . .could not. . .accept that degree of domination from him. It reduced her to a puppet of his will, and her own sense of self-worth demanded more respect from him than that.

'No, Morgan,' she said flatly.

'No?' He sounded disbelieving, as if he couldn't credit having heard the word.

It took all her courage to maintain her stand as his incredulity gave way to glaring fury. 'I'm sorry,' she said with somewhat tremulous determination. 'But I'm staying here until I've finished learning what I have to learn. You never gave me any say in those terms you made, Morgan, so I'm saying this now. I'm not something you can use and dispose of as you see fit.'

His eyes slashed contempt at her, making Kathleen shrivel inside herself. 'It may have escaped your notice, but I have been fulfilling my side of the bargain without complaint or restraint. I expect no less from you. Whether you agreed to them or not, they were—and are—*my terms*.' His voice dropped to a low, threatening note of barely suppressed violence. 'And whatever else there is between us, Kathleen Mavourney, has absolutely no bearing on those terms. If you feel. . .used. . .' he snarled the word '. . .all you have to do is say *no* to my so-called demands. Unlike the terms on which you stay here, by which you get what you want, and I get what I want, anything else is a matter of choice. So don't ever. . .ever. . .attempt to use your body or our relationship as some kind of weapon over me.'

Kathleen shook her head in helpless distress. 'I wouldn't do that, Morgan. I wasn't trying to. I am aware of all you've done for me. I'm not ungrateful. . .' She was sorely tempted to climb down from the stand she had taken. She desperately wanted to please him, to do what he asked, to do anything that would repair this unbearable ruction between them. Yet still some core of self-assertion demanded he recognise her right to her own existence. Her eyes filled with appeal as she uttered the necessary words. 'But I'm not your slave. I'll sing for you. But I won't be ordered around as if——'

She got no further. A furious oath broke from his lips, his arm slashed out in violent dismissal of anything else she might say, and he turned on his heel and left her to her own existence.

Kathleen did not run after him. She couldn't. She was trembling all over. She stood there staring at the empty doorway, her heart pounding with profound agitation as the full realisation of all Morgan had said pressed down on her.

Their relationship meant nothing special to him. She wasn't special to him. Not as a person. Only her voice was of any importance to him. The rest he could dismiss as if it was of no account to him. He was probably deciding right now to terminate any further intimacy between them, if not throw her out altogether. . .like Crystal Carlyle.

Her forehead felt clammy. The hiss of the played-out tape she had been listening to was a mocking reminder of what she had fought for. . .meaningless noise now. . .and meaningless even if she played it through again. Impossible to concentrate on subtle technicalities in her distraught state of mind. She had won nothing by arguing with Morgan. . .and quite possibly she had lost everything.

She blundered over to the hi-fi system to turn all the switches off, too upset to take carefully measured steps and lurching ahead clumsily in her haste. She hated herself; hated the ineptitude that stress invariably brought to her movements; hated the silly pride that had made her seem ungrateful for all Morgan had done for her; hated her stupidity for having hoped their relationship meant as much to him as it did to her.

He had never given her reason to think that. He had never pretended to her. He would have gone to Crystal

Carlyle if she hadn't stopped him, and any hurt resulting from her decision to give freely of herself to Morgan Llewellyn could not be laid at his door. He hadn't forced her. He hadn't demanded it of her. She had taken all that he had offered of himself because she had wanted to.

But the aching misery of knowing it had no real bearing on his life could not be banished by any of the feverish reasoning she applied. Tears stung her eyes and she stumbled her way to the nearest chair, dropped into it, and wept in uncontrollable grief for the delusion that Morgan had stripped of any substance with his brutal candour.

Eventually she mopped up her tears and tried to draw some consolation from the fact that she had kept her self-respect by insisting that he allow her some individual rights. It wasn't that she objected to his terms, but she was not going to be treated like a slave. On the other hand—and to be completely fair about it—since she was no longer doing anything purposeful, she should probably go to him and offer to sing whatever he wanted her to sing. Except that her throat was aching, and she cringed at the thought of facing Morgan's fury again.

A discreet knock on the opened door made her heart leap with apprehension, but it was only Phillips announcing his presence before approaching her with sombre dignity. He stopped three paces away from her, drawing her reluctant attention.

'Yes?' she asked bleakly.

'It is Mr Llewellyn's *request* that when the time is *convenient* to you, Miss Mavourney, you will join him in the music-room.'

Kathleen could hardly believe her ears. 'Would. . .?'

Her throat felt like rough sand-paper. She swallowed hard. 'Would you say that again please, Phillips?'

He repeated the message, word for word.

Kathleen still couldn't believe it. Morgan climbing down? It couldn't be! It had to be blistering sarcasm. Phillips was making the request sound courteous because he would never deliver any message without making it sound polite.

She lifted a look of anxious appeal. 'Is Mr Llewellyn . . .very tetchy. . .at the present moment, Phillips?'

The butler pursed his lips as he gave the matter grave consideration. Kathleen was painfully aware that he would have observed her blotchy cheeks and washed-out eyes. Probably the whole household staff knew by now that there had been a 'scene'.

'No, miss,' came the measured judgement. 'I think "tense" might be a fairer description.' He bent his head towards her and lowered his voice to a conspiratorial level. 'Mr Llewellyn is not always the most patient of men.'

Kathleen heaved a feeling sigh. 'You can say that again, Phillips.'

Another knock on the door distracted his attention. 'Ah. . .here it is!' He straightened as Alice entered, bearing a tray. Phillips gave Kathleen his benevolent smile. 'Tibbet thought a cup of tea. Always calming, a cup of tea.'

'I put the sugar and milk in, miss, so you can drink it straight up,' Alice assured her.

'Thank you,' Kathleen managed huskily, tears welling into her eyes at the caring and thoughtfulness of everyone in this house. Except, of course, for Morgan Llewellyn.

Phillips cleared his throat noisily and Alice beat a hasty retreat. 'No need to drink your tea straight away,' he said with a return to lofty dignity. 'A temperate course if often the wisest.'

He gave her a half-bow and was heading towards the door before Kathleen had recovered her composure. 'Phillips. . .' she called after him. He turned enquiringly. 'Thank you. And please thank Tibbet for me.'

'I will certainly do that, Miss Mavourney,' he replied gravely, and continued on his way.

She drank the tea slowly, warming her throat and easing the tightness there. Morgan wanted her to sing for him and she had to do the best she could or he would think she was cheating him. Phillips' idea of 'tense' probably meant something like a powder keg about to explode. There was only one way to defuse it and that was to give Morgan what he considered his due under the terms of his bargain.

Kathleen put down the empty cup, pushed herself to her feet, took three deep breaths, squared her shoulders, and began the long walk to the music-room. If their personal relationship was over, then it was over, and she had to face that with dignity. She had always known it would end one day. And despite the throbbing pain in her heart she didn't regret the choice she had made. She only wished. . .but there was no point in wishing. There had to be a limit to the miracles in any one person's life.

She reached the door to the music-room. Fear of what waited for her behind it made Kathleen pause for a moment. Then she remembered the way Sister Cecily had fought Morgan for her sake wihtout taking one fearful step backwards. Kathleen stiffened her backbone, lifted her hand, rapped a courtesy knock, then opened the door.

CHAPTER NINE

MORGAN was pounding out Carver's Theme on the piano when Kathleen entered the music-room. The dark fury of the music deepened her apprehension. His eyes glittered a fierce resentment at her when she reached his side. He broke off the theme with a crashing chord, but he made no cutting comment about the timing of her arrival. He made no reference whatsoever to their argument. He simply glowered at her for a moment then nodded to the music-sheets lying on top of the piano.

'This is Lorna's first song,' he said, and his voice was low and tense. 'I'll play it for you so you can fit the words to the music. Then I'll hear you sing it.'

Kathleen could not stop her hands from trembling as she picked up the sheets. Morgan's first composition for Lorna, after all these weeks of working towards it. . .a whole lifetime of working towards it. . .and she had rebuffed him, implied it wasn't important, when he had wanted to test his most critical piece of music on her.

The notes and words swam before her eyes, accusing her of spoiling a moment of sharing that could have been wonderful. There would be no pleasure in it now. No excitement. No joy. Kathleen could not have felt more wretched, but she forced herself to channel all her concentration on to the song, desperate to offer some compensation for making him wait for her convenience.

Morgan had long ago outlined the opening scene to

her: the gathering of the Doone Clan in the great hall to celebrate Sir Ensor Doone's birthday; his son, Carver, sitting on his right, his adopted granddaughter, Lorna, on his left—a rollicking banquet scene that portrayed Ensor's corrupt nobility, and Carver's dark lust for his father's power and Lorna's pure beauty. At this point in the story Lorna was ignorant of her kidnapping and believed Ensor to be her grandfather, Carver her cousin, and she didn't understand why she felt such an alien in the midst of the Doone Clan.

Morgan had entitled the song 'Not One Of Them'. As he played the music through, Kathleen shivered at the uncanny rightness of his interpretation of Lorna's feelings: the sense of bewilderment circling upwards to a desperate need to escape the evil pressing around her, and the soaring plea for a different life that was good, and free of fear.

What Morgan expressed in his music so closely reflected the painful confusion of Kathleen's own feelings that when he started the song a second time it was virtually a release for her to sing the words he had written; she identified so completely with Lorna's emotional turmoil that she ended up with tears in her eyes.

In the silence that followed the last note of the song, Morgan stared at her for an agonisingly long time. He had a strange, remote expression on his face, as if he was not quite seeing her, or not in any sharp focus. Kathleen did not know if she had delivered what he required of her, and at last she couldn't bear his apparent alienation from her.

'Morgan. . .did I sing it. . .was it what you wanted?'

He shook his head. 'Perfect. . .perfect.' He sighed and his mouth twisted in self-mockery. 'All these years. . .wasted. . .fooling myself into being content with less than what I was capable of.'

Again he shook his head. His eyes focused intensely on her, probing, wondering. 'Kathleen, I heard you singing it in my head as I composed that music. But even after all I've heard of your voice, you captured something more. Something so elemental. . .' He gave a harsh laugh. 'That blasted nun, who taught me so much. . .she probably has a grin all over her devilishly cherubic face right now. And I can't even hate her for it.'

Kathleen felt weak with relief. Morgan was not angry with her any more. He was pleased with her. . .or at least pleased with the way she had sung his song. He smiled at her as he rose from the piano stool.

'I've got Lorna now,' he said, and he couldn't keep the triumph out of his voice. 'I knew she was in you, Kathleen. I knew it was only a matter of time and you would give it to me. The purity and the passion. . .' his eyes glittered into hers as he cupped her face in his hands '. . .and the voice. I couldn't bear to have anyone else sing it now. It has to be you. . .your voice. . .the greatest creation I've ever made. . .my Lorna.'

And he kissed her with such deep tenderness that Kathleen once more fell helplessly in thrall to the power he had to draw on her soul. She knew now what her intuition had told her all along; that she was somehow entwined with the music he was composing, that he had used her—without any conscience at all— to take what he wanted or needed from her to create the substance of his dream. He had found *his way* and exploited it ruthlessly. . .yet even knowing all this, beyond any shadow of doubt, Kathleen still melted in response to the seductive softness of his kiss.

She let him lead her to his bed. She let him make slow, exquisite love to her. It didn't feel like being used. It felt almost as if he worshipped her, cherished her, and, although her heart ached for the reality of his truly loving her, she could not reject the dream. It would end soon enough, when the score for *Lorna Doone* was completed. To Morgan's satisfaction. She could not bring herself to end it of her own accord. She loved him. She probably always would. No matter what he did.

She lay with her cheek pressed over his heart. Morgan played with her hair as he invariably did in the peaceful aftermath of lovemaking, weaving it through his fingers and fanning it out in patterns that pleased him. She felt the vibration in his chest before a low harsh laugh spilled from his throat, a guttural sound that was more triumph than amusement.

'We'll intrigue them. We'll make your liability an asset. Then there's no doubt we will win,' he said.

'What do you want to win, Morgan?'

'Interest. Publicity. Speculation. Success. Things don't just happen, Kathleen. You have to make them happen. And I intend to do just that.'

The uncanny repetition of Sister Cecily's words sent a little shiver down her spine. And when Morgan rolled her on to her back and propped himself up on his side his eyes had the same glittering purpose in them. . .a mission that would be accomplished against any odds.

'I'll make you what you deserve to be. What you have to be. And you will be. But first the public will have to be prepared for the break away from all I've ever done before. Curiosity has to be aroused to pave the way for acceptance. A long build-up of stories to whet interest. I'll arrange that.'

He trailed a finger down her cheek. 'And you. . .you will become a star. . .a star the like of which the world has never seen before.'

'*Me*?'

He laughed at the shocked look on her face. 'Of course. Only you. What did you think I was saying earlier? After hearing you sing Lorna, I could never settle for second-best. It has to be *your* Lorna on the recording. And there'll be no question about who you are. You'll be my wife. That's the surest way of making it work.'

The impact of his words crashed through Kathleen like a tidal wave, leaving her breathless and speechless. She stared up at him, half fearful that she had got it wrong. She was dazed enough by Morgan's intention to make her a recording star. But. . .his wife!

His mouth curled into a sardonic quirk. 'Don't give me any argument about this not being your life's work. *Lorna Doone* is meant to appeal to more popular taste than grand opera, but remember, I composed it for your voice. If Kiri Te Kanawa can sing Maria's part in *West Side Story*, you can sing my Lorna.'

Kathleen tried to get her tongue and throat working again. She could only manage to produce one word. 'Wife?'

He grinned. 'It gives you instant celebrity. Black Morgan finally succumbs. Confirmed bachelor and man-about-town totally entranced by latest discovery. Lorna composed especially for her voice. The public will lap it up. It'll be the Wedding of the Year.'

Kathleen was in absolute turmoil. Morgan was proposing to marry her for a publicity stunt. A totally cynical promotional exercise. Nothing to do with loving her or wanting to share the rest of his life with her. But a treacherous little hope whispered that he had never married any other woman, and that their relationship would last a lot longer than she had ever anticipated if she became his wife. He did seem to love her voice. It wasn't entirely impossible that he should come to love her. . .in time.

On the other hand, perhaps he would take it for granted that he could completely dominate her life if he were her husband. How much would he expect from her in return for stardom and the status of his wife? Would he dismiss her ambitions if they were not tied to his?

Amusement danced in his eyes. 'Nothing to say, Kathleen?'

She hastily worked some moisture into her mouth and forced herself to voice the doubt uppermost in her mind. 'I'm not sure about marrying you, Morgan. What kind of terms do you have in mind for that?'

He frowned at her, obviously put out that she should raise any issue over his master-plan. 'The same as we have now, of course. We'll have to do some mixing around. Be seen together. Make you a mystery girl to start with. Start everyone wondering just who Kathleen Mavourney is.' His face cleared to a broad grin. 'It'll be fun. We'll take a trip to Paris. Fit you out in beautiful clothes. Simple classical stuff that will highlight your hair. You'd enjoy that, wouldn't you?'

Reason still kept pointing out it was all a publicity angle, but the twinkling invitation in Morgan's eyes was an irresistible temptation. Kathleen was only human, and what Morgan was offering appealed as strongly to her feminine heart as it did to her ambitious dreams; beautiful clothes, being paired with him in public and private, his wife, his new singing star, her voice recorded on discs and tapes and records which would be played all around the world.

'Yes. I'd like that,' she acknowledged huskily. It wasn't the kind of marriage she had dreamed of, hoped for, but Morgan would be her husband for a while anyway. Which was more than Crystal Carlyle had ever managed.

'And I shall enjoy showing you off to the world. My Lorna Doone,' he said, and kissed her with exultant possessiveness.

For the first time since they had become lovers, Kathleen couldn't respond whole-heartedly to Morgan's kiss. If he had said 'my Kathleen', or 'my wife-to-be', or anything else but 'my Lorna Doone', she would not have felt any inhibition. But somehow it didn't feel as if he was really kissing her, but his creation, and it made her wonder if Kathleen Mavourney actually existed at all in his mind. Or if Morgan Llewellyn was just Macchiavelli in disguise.

Yet the niggle was quickly drowned in the pleasure of the hours that followed his twofold proposal of fame and marriage. Morgan was as overpowering in triumphant happiness as he was in towering anger. They had a celebration dinner, drank champagne, and Kathleen basked in the blissful warmth of his approval and delight in her, even if he was only seeing her as 'his Lorna Doone'. Never had he been so charming to her, so caring about what she would like to have and do, so vital and handsome. . .and she loved him.

The next morning Morgan accompanied her to London but he did not come in to her lesson with Madame Desfarges. He had business elsewhere. However, he assured her he would be back in time to pick her up by the end of the hour. He did, in fact, enter Madame's music studio just as the singing teacher was telling Kathleen that her name had been entered into the European Eisteddfod to be held in Paris in two months' time.

'You have not qualified through the English Zone, but I have managed to bypass that formality,' Madame declared. 'It is enough that I have asked for you to be heard. So we have two months to prepare for——'

'No!'

Morgan's emphatic interjection startled Kathleen, but Madame Desfarges turned on him in incredulous affront.

'Mr Llewellyn, our agreement was that you do not interfere with——'

He cut in with ruthless deliberation. 'Not this year, *madame*. We both know why you've used your influence to enter Kathleen into that Eisteddfod. You think she will win her nominated section. And so do I. And that will bring publicity. The wrong kind of publicity.'

Madame Desfarges threw her hands up in denouncement. 'Are you mad? It will be the beginning of making her name! The right people——'

'The wrong people!' Morgan sliced back. 'Kathleen will be labelled as the type of singer that most people have no interest in. Not only no interest, but they will be actively turned off by the suggestion of something too highbrow for them to enjoy. I will not allow that to happen. Not when there's so much riding on it.'

'Morgan. . .' Kathleen began pleadingly.

'And precisely what is riding on it, Mr Llewellyn? This is her life's work. Nothing is more important!' Madame proclaimed in outraged indignation.

'*My* life's work is riding on it, *madame*!' Morgan snapped at her, then turned quickly to Kathleen. 'Not this year! Next year it won't matter, but it can't be this year, Kathleen.'

'Your life's work!' Madame squawked contemptuously. 'Trite little popular tunes——'

'Don't pre-judge, *madame*! You've already made one grievous error on that score,' Morgan shot at her venomously. 'What I've composed for Kathleen's voice is on a scale far different from all my previous work. And I will not have its acceptance compromised by you or anyone else. Kathleen's début as a singer will be with my music, and I shall orchestrate that début for maximum impact.'

The Frenchwoman was not the least bit appeased. 'You will ruin her!' she accused in bitter condemnation.

'I will make her!' Morgan retorted fiercely. 'And let me remind you, *madame*, it did not hurt John McCormick to sing "Galway Bay". Nor did it hurt Dame Nellie Melba to sing "Home Sweet Home". We need a singer of Kathleen's quality to make a place for great music in popular culture.'

'So!' Madame Desfarges sneered. 'You want to take culture to the masses!'

Kathleen held her breath as Morgan looked about to savage the woman. The black aura of violence around him at that moment was so vibrant that even Madame Desfarges drew herself up sharply, instinctively reacting to danger. But when Morgan spoke it was not with white-heat. His voice was ice-cold steel.

'*Madame*, without the masses. . .there is no culture.' He turned his head slowly to Kathleen. 'We do it my way. Because I say so. And that's the way it's going to be. I will not discuss the matter any further. Come! We're leaving!'

He held out his hand to her. Kathleen was in a hopeless quandary. How could she leave Madame Desfarges on this note? Yet Morgan was demanding she show her loyalty to him. And he was right. About his music for *Lorna Doone*.

Apart from which, he was in no mood to be defied. There was no telling how he might react if she did not go along with him. It was not beyond possibility that he would cut her off from Madame Desfarges altogether. And Kathleen couldn't let that happen.

'I'll see you tomorrow, *madame*,' she said, and as she moved to Morgan's side and took his hand she flashed her teacher a look which pleaded that she desist from any further argument.

'Yes,' the Frenchwoman snapped. 'We shall see.'

Those last three words were a grim challenge to Morgan Llewellyn, and her whole demeanour bespoke a steely determination to flout his edict if she could find some way around it.

Kathleen had the uncomfortable sensation of being the bone between two wolves that would fight to the death before taking a backward step. Neither Morgan nor Madame Desfarges was concerned about what Kathleen herself thought or wanted. Both were motivated by their own strong self-interest. But, however much of themselves they had invested in her, they didn't have the right to think they owned her. And Kathleen silently determined to take control of her own life and do what she wanted to do.

Morgan's black mood was not conducive to reasonable conversation so Kathleen kept silent as they travelled out of London. She had plenty to think about. As deeply as she loved him, Kathleen knew that she would not be content to play second fiddle to Morgan's needs and desires for the rest of her life. Particularly if that meant suppressing her own ambition. It would hurt to leave him. It would hurt to leave the Hermitage and the position he had given her there. Perhaps it would not become necessary, but if it did. . .

And it was best to start asserting herself now while Morgan was a captive audience in the car. However angry he was, he could not walk away from her here. She glanced at the darkly brooding man beside her. Her heart twisted in painful protest at her decision, but Kathleen had not suffered all she had to come this far, only to be trampled underfoot by Morgan Llewellyn or anyone else.

'Morgan. . .'

He turned his head sharply towards her, ruthless determination carved into every line of his face. 'It'll ruin everything, Kathleen. It can't be done. Surely *you* can see that!' he said tersely.

'Yes. I don't deny your point of view, and I'll ask Madame Desfarges to withdraw my name,' she said evenly. 'But unless I can show her that it's the right thing to do, she might wash her hands of me. And I don't want that, Morgan. She's too good a teacher for me to lose. If I took Lorna's song with me tomorrow and——'

'I don't have to prove anything to that woman!' he grated, his face hardening to stony pride.

'No. You don't have to,' Kathleen agreed, hating the dark glasses he wore as her eyes sought to plead her own cause. 'But it would make things a great deal easier for me to continue learning from Madame Desfarges if she's convinced it won't be doing my name any injury to sing your music.'

His mouth tightened into a grim line and Kathleen's heart sank as he turned away from her. But her mind relentlessly reasoned that, if Morgan could not concede to her need on this point, any feeling he had for her was completely and utterly selfish.

His silence goaded her into a more open rebellion against her dependence on him. 'The prize money, if I won that section of the Eisteddfod, would keep me for a year, Morgan,' she stated pointedly.

That jerked his gaze back to her. 'You have some complaint about the way you're kept?' he bit out acidly.

'You think I enjoy being a kept woman when you make me feel I have no choices of my own? That everything has to be on your terms?' she retorted bitterly. 'You've got what you wanted from me, Morgan. You said as much yesterday. You've got your return for keeping me. And making me your recording star is what *you* want, so don't say you're doing it for me. It's not for me. If it suited you to use Crystal Carlyle's voice instead of mine, you'd do precisely that.'

He shook his head in angry incredulity. 'Crystal? Are you mad? You know damned well that I composed for your voice!'

'And I'll sing for you,' Kathleen said grimly. 'But not at the cost of being cut off from what I want, Morgan. I'm not asking much. You don't have to come with me to my lesson tomorrow. Just let me take the song——'

'No!' The vehement negative exploded any chance of reaching a reasonable compromise.

Her face grew pale and pinched as she faced up to the inescapable truth. Her eyes were a bleak wash of pain. 'You don't care about me at all, do you? The only thing that matters to you is having your own way,' she said tonelessly, and turned away from him, fighting to hold back a threatening well of tears.

She was not going to cry. It could only shame her in the face of Morgan's indifference. Her fingers began a frantic pleating of her skirt as she struggled to keep her composure. Her whole body ached with the tension of holding in the emotions that Morgan would only despise.

'Kathleen. . .'

It was a gravelled sigh of exasperation. She would not, could not look at him. A hand reached over and stopped the nervous scrabble of her fingers, squeezing them tightly within his warm grasp.

'I'll come with you tomorrow and we'll stuff Lorna's song down Madame Desfarges' throat. If that doesn't shut her up I might very well strangle her. But if you think it's worth that risk, I'll try it. For you. And that's more than I'd do for anyone else, Kathleen.'

His tone was grudgingly indulgent. Kathleen wanted to believe he cared about her, but reason insisted that once again he was only protecting his own interests, making sure he kept her co-operation with his plans.

'Thank you,' she said stiffly, still not looking at him. There was one other consideration he had overlooked in his ungracious concession. Of course it meant nothing to him. But it did to her. It meant a great deal to her in terms of personal freedom. However humiliating it was to bring the subject up, she felt entitled to do so in her present circumstances.

'I don't know what you pay your recording artists, Morgan, but I want to be paid the same sum I might have won if I'd sung in the Eisteddfod,' she said in a tight little voice. 'I know you intend buying me clothes and taking me places, but that's part of the publicity you want. I would like to earn some money of my own. That I'm not beholden to you for.'

'Beholden?' His hand released hers, lifting quickly to her chin. Before Kathleen could take any evasive action he jerked her head around to face him. He was frowning hard. 'Anything I have is yours,' he said forcefully. 'I thought that was understood, Kathleen. As my wife——'

'I don't want your money, Morgan,' she cried, wenching her chin out of his grasp, her eyes cold with the proud need for independence. 'I just want what's due to me. Not as your wife. As a person who's done a job of work for you. Like any other singer. Money that I'm entitled to because I earned it.'

He shook his head, not understanding until enlightenment slowly dawned. 'Kathleen, haven't you got any money?'

Embarrassment sent a surge of burning colour to her cheeks. 'Not much. And I don't want you to give me any,' she added fiercely as he reached for his wallet. 'If you pay me when I do the recording, that's all I ask.'

His mouth turned down into a grimace of self-disgust. 'I'll see to it as soon as we get home.'

'I don't want——'

'For God's sake!' he cut in explosively. But he said no more. With an angry frown he turned away and retreated into a black brooding silence that accompanied him all the way home.

It was hopeless. . .stupid to be clutching at straws, Kathleen railed at herself. There was no way to protect herself from Morgan's domination except to leave him. Nothing was going to change. He didn't want to listen to her, didn't want to see any other point of view but his own. He might make a few grudging concessions now and then because he needed her for his music, but he didn't love her. Didn't care what she thought or felt. He kept her and he would marry her to suit his purpose, and the longer she stayed with him, the more he would undermine any chance she had of being independent of him.

She couldn't go through with the charade of marriage that he had proposed. It would only put her further and further in his debt, and the price he would exact from her was too high. If he had loved her she would have done anything for him, but she couldn't fool herself about that any longer.

Slowly but surely Kathleen formed her resolution. She would stay with Morgan until he had finished composing the music for Lorna. She owed him that much. But she was not going to ride to fame on his coat-tails. Any name she earned in the music world had to be on her own merits or it wasn't worth anything. She would take her chances at the Eisteddfod. And if she failed. . .well, she simply wasn't good enough to make it on her own.

They arrived back at the Hermitage and Morgan finally stirred himself to speak to Kathleen as he helped her out of the car. 'I'll talk to Tibbet,' he said gruffly. 'She'll set up a private account for you. Arrange credit cards. You will never want for anything again, Kathleen.'

'Thank you,' she murmured, mortified by his generosity but too sick at heart to argue about anything. It wasn't money that she wanted from him. His wealth, his position, his power to make his own way. . .none of those things could ever keep her with him now. She would only take whatever funds she needed to tide her over when she left him. And she would pay every penny back as soon as she could.

'You needn't come with me tomorrow, Morgan,' she said as they walked up the steps. 'You're quite right. You don't have to prove anything to Madame Desfarges. Your music will speak for itself soon enough.'

'But what about you?' he asked, throwing her a look of concern.

Kathleen shook her head. 'I don't think Madame will give me up. And she ought to have some respect for my judgement of music by now. I'll tell her that what you've composed for Lorna is so beautiful it'll make her head spin.'

Morgan's black mood cleared and he gave a satisfied laugh. 'Let's hope I can keep the standard up for the rest.'

He put his arm around her shoulders and hugged her close to him. A bittersweet pleasure flooded through Kathleen. She wondered if she would ever stop loving him. . .wanting him.

An ironic little smile softened her mouth. In one sense she would always be a part of him. Without her he would never have composed *Lorna Doone*. And that was too important a goal for her to disturb him now by revealing her intentions. When he had all the music. . .then she would tell him.

CHAPTER TEN

OVER the next few weeks Morgan worked obsessively on his creation, driven by a white-hot energy that increased as he built from one magically moving song to the next. And, while he shared his excitement at each success with Kathleen, it only made her more and more conscious that it was his music he loved.

During this important period in his life, Kathleen was an extension of his music. She understood that. And she gave him whatever he wanted or needed for the fulfilment of his dream. Not by word or deed did she raise one quarrelsome note in their relationship. There was so little time left together, and this was her gift to him for all he had given her.

Sadly but firmly Kathleen set about planning her own future. Madame Desfarges could not readily accept Kathleen's insistence that Morgan's music was of a standard worthy of her pupil's voice, but the issue was promptly dropped with Kathleen's decision to sing in the Eisteddfod. Once the situation was explained to her, the Frenchwoman offered various helpful suggestions that assured Kathleen of some secure backing when she made the move that had to come.

'You have a talent that must not be lost to the world!' Madame declared with deep personal conviction. 'If need be, I shall foster it myself. But success will come.' She looked down her long haughty nose and added with some asperity, 'You do not need Morgan Llewellyn for that!'

But Kathleen silently grieved that she would not be

singing *Lorna Doone* for Morgan. She loved all the songs he composed for her. At last the only one left to be completed to his satisfaction was the climactic wedding trio where the three protagonists—Carver Doone, John Ridd, and Lorna—sang their separate themes together as Lorna, in her white bridal gown, walked down the aisle towards her husband-to-be, and Carver lurked in the gallery above, waiting to shoot her.

'I need all the voices!' Morgan muttered in frustration as he adjusted the phrasing for John Ridd and Carver for the umpteenth time. 'I'll ask them to come for a trial run. On Sunday afternoon.'

'Ask whom?' Kathleen prompted nervously. The secret mission she had set herself would be over as soon as Morgan had this music right. She would be free to leave. Free to do what she had to do. . .without him. But it was difficult to ignore the pain in her heart as she waited to hear what he planned for Sunday afternoon. Would that be the last day?

Morgan frowned as he named the tenor and the baritone in his current stage production. 'They'll have to be sworn to secrecy about you, Kathleen,' he added, shooting her a look that commanded compliance to his judgement. 'I don't want the story to break yet.'

Which was just as well, Kathleen thought in uneasy relief. She didn't want any story to break either. Particularly if it was inaccurate and embarrassing to Morgan.

Colin Harlech was a fine tenor whom Morgan had in mind to cast as John Ridd; and the baritone, Adrian Foster, had the voice and the dark, heavy looks which were well suited to Carver's role. Both men were experienced professional singers and they eyed Kathleen with considerable curiosity since she was a total unknown. Morgan rehearsed the two men until they were confident of singing their parts in the trio. Kathleen needed no practice. She knew her part from having sung it many times over for Morgan's satisfaction.

'OK! We'll put it together,' he finally announced.

It began with Carver's music, and Adrian Foster imbued his words with a low, vibrant evil. Then Colin Harlech joined in with John Ridd's pure yearning for his bride. When her cue came, Kathleen lifted her voice high above theirs in a crystal-clear lilt of almost incredulous happiness. She had barely sung beyond her first line when the two men stopped singing and stared at her. She faltered to a halt and looked questioningly at Morgan, sure she had done nothing wrong.

His eyes danced at her in unholy amusement. 'Shall we start again, gentlemen?' he asked good-humouredly. 'A bit more concentration this time?'

'We'll try, Morgan!' Colin said drily. 'But you shouldn't surprise us like this. Mind if we hear Lorna through first? Then we might be able to concentrate.'

'How about twice?' Adrian rumbled. 'My mind has just been blown.'

Kathleen flushed with pleasure as she realised they had stopped to listen to her, that these two men who worked with singers all the time were actually stunned by the quality of her voice. And Morgan was grinning from ear to ear as he asked her to comply with their request.

Working with them for the rest of the afternoon was a deep joy to Kathleen. It was precisely the kind of thing she had dreamed of: hearing her voice combining with others to add that extra element of vivid life to great music. And it was great! Morgan taped the final session and, when he played it back to them, they were all awed by the emotional and dramatic tapestry of sound that had been woven together.

'This is a winner, Morgan. Big!' Colin commented with decisive certainty.

'Mind-blowing!' Adrian asserted.

Morgan smiled at Kathleen, and it was a moment of intimate sharing that she knew she would never forget. It was a silent acknowledgement of the part she had played in drawing his music from him, and she hugged that knowledge to her heart. It was done now—the last composition he had needed for his new and revolutionary creation to be complete—and he didn't need her any more.

Many hours later, in the darkness of the night, she held him cradled in her arms, loving him with her body. . .for the last time. She tried her utmost to keep the sadness at bay but she couldn't banish the sick hollowness that crept into her stomach in the aftermath of their final union. She couldn't imagine a better lover than Morgan. Everything about him stirred an intense sensual pleasure. . .and a terrible yearning for this closeness to continue forever.

'Tomorrow I'll start on the orchestration,' he said, his voice low and rich with satisfaction.

'Yes,' she whispered.

Tomorrow morning was the right time to tell him, she thought. It would spoil this last night with him if she disclosed her plans now. Better to wait until she was ready to go. Make the break quick and clean. And the orchestration would push her out of his mind, once he got over his frustratin of not getting his way over the recording. He would realise, soon enough, that there were other, better-known singers who could do Lorna for him. His music would carry any of them.

He fell asleep before she did. Kathleen lay awake for a long time; holding him, softly caressing him, storing away the memories that had to last her a lifetime. It was late when she woke the next morinng, and Morgan was already gone from her bed.

Kathleen ordered breakfast to be brought to her room. She wasted no time in starting to pack all her belongings.

The sight of Kathleen's suitcases and the obvious evidence of what she was doing brought a puzzled frown to Alice's face when she wheeled in the breakfast trolley. 'Going on a trip, miss?'

'Yes, Alice,' Kathleen answered briefly.

'Would you like me to pack for you, miss?'

'No, thank you, Alice. I'd rather do it myself.'

'As you say, miss,' came the uncertain answer.

Within ten minutes of the maid's departure, Tibbet presented herself. Kathleen was forcing herself to eat a croissant and she asked Tibbet to join her at the table, knowing that she needed and had to ask for the woman's full co-operation if her planned schedule was to work with smooth efficiency.

'Mr Llewellyn did not inform me you were going on a trip, Miss Mavourney,' Tibbet said in questioning concern. 'Can I be of any assistance?'

Kathleen gave her a rueful smile. 'The truth is that I'm leaving the Hermitage, Tibbet. I wish I could stay. Everyone has been so kind to me, and I'll miss you all very much. But I must go, and I must leave this morning. . .'

'Mr Llewellyn. . .'

'Wants me to do something I can't do, Tibbet. I've made the only choice that can be right for me. And my singing career. Mr Llewellyn won't like it, but I have to go. I'd appreciate it if you could help me get my bags to the car before I give him my decision. It'll make things easier. I should be ready by ten o'clock.'

Kathleen managed to keep her gaze steady as the older woman searched her eyes in obvious distress. 'Are you sure this decision is necessary, Miss Mavourney?'

Kathleen's mouth twisted in bitter irony. 'Believe me, Tibbet. I wouldn't do this if there was any other way. You must know that Mr Llewellyn only recognises his own. . .needs. I believe that there are people who even call him Black Morgan. Although I'm not one of them,' she added hastily.

Tibbet heaved a disappointed sigh. 'We will all be very sorry to see you go, Miss Mavourney. But I shall do as you ask.'

'Thank you, Tibbet,' Kathleen murmured in grateful relief for the other woman's understanding. 'And please, thank everyone for all they've done for me.'

Tibbet nodded sadly. She left without any further questions or comment.

Kathleen had a little weep. She had felt so at home here. It tore her heart to walk away from it all. But now was not the time for any weakness. She gathered up her resolution again and went on with the packing.

For the first time since she and Morgan had become lovers, Kathleen pinned up her hair. She chose to wear the green suit and the Paisley silk blouse which were still her best clothes. Somehow it lent more steel to her purpose. . .a superficial pretence that her stay here had changed nothing. She would leave as she had come. . .venturing once more into the unknown with only her courage to support her.

Her suitcases were collected by the chauffeur at ten o'clock. He informed her that the car was waiting at the front steps for her convenience.

Kathleen took one last look at the Blue Room, then started downstairs. She moved slowly. It seemed important to imprint everything on her memory; the pattern of the carpet, the paintings on the walls, the architectural details that Tibbet had pointed out to her when they had first mounted these stairs together—a lifetime ago.

Phillips had stationed himself at the foot of the staircase. He did not look up at her. He made no sign that he was aware of her descent. But the moment she reached his side he turned with his solemn half-bow and addressed her in a low ponderous voice.

'I regret to inform you, Miss Mavourney, that Mr Llewellyn is otherwise engaged at the moment. Miss Carlyle arrived some ten minutes ago. Mr Llewellyn had just gone into the drawing-room to speak to her.'

Crystal! Kathleen's heart sank. Yet. . .perhaps it was best this way. . .to leave him with the kind of woman who typified his world.

Phillips' eyebrows angled down in sympathetic concern. 'If you'll forgive the presumption, Miss Mavourney, I thought perhaps the saloon might be best for a private talk. I could ask Mr Llewellyn——'

'No. . .' She forced a stiff little smile. 'No, it's all right, Phillips. Thank you, but it doesn't really matter.'

His face unexpectedly creased in deep anxiety. 'Miss Mavourney. . .'

Kathleen reached out impulsively and squeezed the old man's hand in affectionate reassurance. 'I'll see Mr Llewellyn in the drawing-room.'

She turned away, moving as fast as she could as she blinked back another rush of tears. She could not cry now. Certainly not in front of Crystal Carlyle. What she had to do had to be done quickly, and with calm dignity. Blindly impelled to get the agony over and

lone with, Kathleen did not knock on the door to the
drawing-room. She had barely begun to push the door
open when she had second thoughts about the wisdom
of her chosen course.

'Liar!'

The passionate outrage in Crystal Carlyle's voice
brought back a host of nasty memories. Kathleen's
hand froze on the doorknob.

'You promised *me* the part, Morgan. Don't think for
one moment that I'll sit still while you hand it to
someone else! I'll teach you a lesson you'll never
forget! The Duke of Penmara wants to marry me. And
'll do that. I'll walk right off your show and out of the
contract. Unless you change your mind. . .'

'Go ahead! Do it!' Morgan invited tonelessly. 'I like
the idea. We couldn't get better publicity. The star of
my new show will be a duchess. Yes, that's excellent.'

The cynicism so implicit in Morgan's reply was a
painful echo of his proposal of marriage to Kathleen.
It stiffened her resolution. She pushed the door open
and stepped inside the room. Neither of the occupants
noticed her entry.

'The star?' Crystal's blistering anger lost some of its
fire, but the belligerent pose she struck in front of
Morgan still challenged him.

He was sprawled in the corner of one of the sofas,
completely unperturbed by his leading lady's show of
temperament. 'Regardless of what you heard from
Colin or Adrian, Crystal, you are certainly in line for
the stage-show,' he assured her blandly.

'But the recording. . .'

'Is not negotiable.' He suddenly spotted Kathleen
and a look of sardonic amusement lightened his
expression as he rose to his feet. 'In fact, if you want

to meet the *Lorna Doone* who sang yesterday, just
turn around, Crystal, and I'll introduce you.'

The woman spun on her heel, a spitting cat ready to
claw anyone who challenged her supremacy. 'You?'
she sneered incredulously.

'No,' Kathleen answered with quiet emphasis. She
shifted her gaze to Morgan and addressed him before
Crystal recollected herself. 'You have the music you
wanted, Morgan. No one can ever deny your great
talent as a composer now. I've only come in to thank
you for my singing lessons. And to say goodbye.'

'Goodbye?' His face stiffened with disbelief.

'I can't be your *Lorna Doone*,' Kathleen stated
flatly. 'I want to be myself. . . Kathleen Mavourney
. . .and that's what I'm going to be. I wish you well,
Morgan. . .always,' she added, her voice breaking
slightly as sadness overwhelmed her.

'Kathleen!'

The violent protest that burst from him jolted her
legs into action. She couldn't bear any argument. She
turned back to the domed hallway, desperately intent
on leaving as fast as possible.

'Let her go, Morgan. She's a nothing!'

'For God's sake, Crystal! Get out of my way!'

'No! Stay with me. I'm better for you than she is.
She's only a witch!'

There was the sound of a scuffle. Something crashing. A desperate cry of 'Kathleen!' and then a frenzied
scream.

Phillips was at the front door. Kathleen threw him a
hunted look of appeal and he wordlessly responded,
opening the door for her to leave.

The last words she heard were from Morgan, furious
with frustration. 'Damn you, Crystal! Damn you to
hell!'

Phillips obligingly closed the door behind Kathleen, protecting her from any further distress. The black Rolls-Royce was waiting, the passenger door already open for her. Whether the butler had made some signal to the chauffeur, Kathleen didn't know, but as she hurried awkwardly across the porch the chauffeur bounded up the steps to take her arm and help her down to the car.

The moment she was settled in the back seat Kathleen shut her eyes tight and prayed hard. She couldn't bear it if Morgan tried to stop her now. She heard the engine purr into life and the car started to move. There was no sound of pursuit. No command to halt. The car picked up pace and the dreadful thrumming of her heart eased a little.

Frustration was all Morgan would feel over her departure from his life, Kathleen thought in abject misery. The blackest of black frustrations. Nothing else. Nothing like the pain that was coursing through her.

He had his music. And he would find a way to get whatever else he wanted. But not through her. She would not be used like that again. Not even for the man she loved. She had her own life to live, a dream to pursue, and the tears that kept welling into her eyes would eventually dry up. . .in time.

CHAPTER ELEVEN

KATHLEEN had not expected the almost military precision with which Madame Desfarges whisked her out of London. No sooner had Morgan's chauffeur driven the Rolls-Royce away than Kathleen's luggage was stowed in Madame's Citroën and they were on their way.

'I do not trust that man to accept anything that goes against his wishes,' the Frenchwoman declared, casting a frowning look at the pale face of her protégée. The ravages made by a storm of tears were all too obvious, and left little doubt about the depth of Kathleen's vulnerability where Morgan Llewellyn was concerned. 'You will be safe from any pressures at my farmhouse in Brittany,' she added with satisfaction.

'It's very good of you,' Kathleen murmured, and listened passively to all the arrangements Madame Desfarges had made for her, automatically agreeing that it was best she remain out of Morgan's reach for as long as possible.

They took the channel ferry to Saint-Malo, then travelled on by car to virtually the westernmost tip of Brittany. The farmhouse was just outside the fishing village of Pont-Croix and was situated on a bluff overlooking the ocean. It was dark by the time they arrived so the vantage-point made no impact on Kathleen.

They were greeted by a middle-aged couple who ran the farm and looked after the house for Madame

Desfarges. A meal was ready for them. The bedrooms had been aired. A fire was burning in the living-room.

Kathleen was so exhausted by the emotional and physical stress of the long day that she found it difficult to follow the French being spoken. The dialect sounded faintly Germanic, and in the end she gave up trying to understand and simply nodded to all speech directed at her.

She followed Gaston Millot as he carried her bags up to her bedroom. This was pleasantly rustic; exposed beams on the ceiling, heavy, practical furniture, and a pretty patchwork quilt on the bed. The fittings in the bathroom next door were old-fashioned but more than adequate for her needs. The house was a far cry from the splendours of the Hermitage, but Kathleen thought it had a cosy, relaxing atmosphere as she rejoined Madame Desfarges in the living-room.

'It was as well we left when we did,' Madame remarked when Kathleen was comfortably settled in an armchair. 'I have been on the telephone to London. Morgan Llewellyn chased after you, arriving barely ten minutes after we departed. He frightened my maid with the violence of his temper, bursting into the house and searching the rooms. Refusing to leave until he was sure you were not there. He was accompanied by a woman who also seemed to have no control over her temper.'

Crystal. . .still fighting for her rights, Kathleen thought wearily. She vaguely remembered a red sports car parked in the driveway of the Hermitage this morning, and could only wonder what had happened to prevent Morgan from not catching up with the Rolls-Royce. Kathleen was grateful for whatever had delayed him.

'I'm sorry, *madame*,' she said with a pained grimace.

'I hope Mr Llewellyn doesn't give you any more trouble on my account.'

Madame Desfarges sniffed. 'I am not easily intimidated, Kathleen. Should he make a return visit, he will not get past me. But I think it wise if you stay here until I advise you otherwise. A rest will do you good. And there is still a month before the Eisteddfod.'

Kathleen nodded, too drained to even think about what she should do. She had carried out her resolution. Somehow she had managed to get through this day and tomorrow it would be easier. Surely every day that went on had to become easier. They had to be or she could not bear it. There had to come a time when she would dredge up the strength to rededicate herself to her own career. And then Morgan wouldn't matter so much.

Madame Desfarges returned to London the next morning, leaving Kathleen in the care of the Millot family. Gaston and Lucille were pleasant and obliging, but Kathleen mostly kept herself to herself. She did not want company. The void in her heart was too deep.

The days slipped by, one barely distinguishable from another. One morning Gaston drove her to Pont-Croix in his truck and she sat at one of the tables of a pavement café for an hour or so, watching the fishermen mend their nets. Most afternoons she spent sitting on a wooden garden-bench on top of the bluff beyond the farmhouse. The view was restful and never boring.

The ocean was rarely empty of some boat or other, and, even if it was, the changing colours of the water and sky were fascinating enough. Sometimes a mist rolled in, gradually swallowing up everything. Kathleen liked watching that.

It was on one such afternoon that Morgan found her. Kathleen rose from her bench, the cold dampness of the air persuading her it was time to return to the farmhouse. She did not want to catch a chill. She had to protect her voice for the coming competition.

She turned to take the path back to the house. Her heart caught painfully at the sight of a man in black striding towards her. She pushed back the red swathes of hair that the wind had whipped across her face and focused on him with intense concentration, not believing the image that was so irrevocably stamped on her mind.

It could not be him. . .and yet how could it not be? She knew every line of that powerful body which was unmistakably emphasised by the black sweater and jeans. And no one else emanated such ferocity of feeling with every purposeful step taken. He wore no dark glasses but the light had been softened by the mist. He would not need them.

Fear churned through her in sickening waves. How had he found her? Had he done something dreadful to Madame Desfarges? Why did he have to make it so hard for her? How was she going to turn away from him again?

And beneath the fear was such a deep undercurrent of yearning that Kathleen could do nothing but stand there and wait for him to reach her. She ached with a terrible weakness. Her skin was clammy. Her eyes clung feverishly to the face which grew more sharply defined as he quickly closed the distance between them.

His skin looked tightly stretched over the angular lines of cheek and jaw, as if he was strained to the limit of endurance. His mouth was a grim slash, echoing the ruthless cut of his chin. His black hair was feathered across his forehead by the wind, adding a further element of wildness to his appearance, and the deadly intent of his approach. And his eyes—those dark, brilliant eyes—burned with so many volatile emotions that Kathleen's heart kicked into nervous panic.

He came to an abrupt halt barely two paces from her, his chest heaving, his hands clenching tightly at his sides. Kathleen could feel the intense despair and desire swirling around her, tying her to him more surely than any physical embrace.

'Kathleen. . .' The whisper of a plea, a darkly gravelled need, but still the surge of command that could not be tempered by any control at all. . .threaded with desperation yet clawing to dominate. . .to take and hold and bend to his will.

'I don't want to live without you. I can't live without you,' he said with a vehemence that punched the words into her mind. 'If I can't have you. . .you cannot conceive the hell I live through. . .my darling girl. . . I might as well be dead. For all the good I am to anyone, I might as well be.'

He was doing it to her again, using the power of his need to bind her to him! And his power was so formidable that she could barely find the strength to break away, to regather her reeling mind and grasp the will to fight for her own survival, to resist what she had to resist. She wrenched her gaze from his and stared out at the ocean. . .the mist writhing against the white crests of the waves.

'I gave you all I could, Morgan.' Her voice sounded so thin. Her throat was thick, choked with her own ravening need for him. She forced some sternness of soul into it. 'You want. . .too much! You take. . .too much!'

'No. . .no. . .it won't be like that! Not this time. I'll do whatever I have to do for you, Kathleen. Whatever you want, whatever your needs are, I'll live by them.

Because you're more important to me than anything else.'

She flashed him a look of scathing disbelief and almost succumbed to the burning purpose that radiated from him. Then she remembered the obsessive way he had gone after his music, the blindness with which he shut out everything else. . .until he had what he wanted.

'That's not true, Morgan,' she said harshly. 'I know you too well now. You'll do and say whatever you have to until I give in. That's what this is all about. To get what you want.'

'It's what you want too, Kathleen!' he fired back at her, his eyes blazing with intense passion. 'And I won't let you deny that!'

He stepped forward and swept her into a fiercely possessive embrace, so crushingly close that the shudder than ran through him vibrated through her body.

'I swore I wouldn't do this to you. . . I swore I'd let you choose freely. . .but I can't! I can't let you go. I can't let you leave me.'

Kathleen was helpless against his iron-like strength and her body played traitor to her will, responding eagerly as his hands moved over her; feverishly kneading, stroking, clutching, igniting the same urgency of desire that flowed so forcefully from him. His mouth swept through her tangled hair, punctuating each passionate burst of speech with hungry kisses.

'Tell me you love me. Tell me it wasn't for the music. Tell me you gave what you gave me because you had to. . .because it was right. . .because it was me. . .and you need me as much as I need you.'

Confusion swirled through her mind. Her heart was pumping so chaotically that she couldn't think. All she

knew was that Morgan was demanding. . .and she had
to fight his demands. . .had to. . .

'Kiss me,' he begged hoarsely. 'I'll go mad if I can't
have you, Kathleen. I don't care about anything else.
Only you. . .'

Her lips quivered, unable to form the words to stop
him regardless of the frightened dictates of her mind.
His lips found hers on a gentle moan, covered them,
seduced them into surrender, and the ravening need
she had tried so hard to hold back devoured all sanity
as his mouth invaded hers. She matched his passionate
greed for the intimacy they had shared with a wild lust
that ripped through every layer of civilised thought or
behaviour. Their kiss was one of attack and plunder
and fierce, primitive possession, overwhelming any
sense of separate existence.

Morgan's hands raked up through her hair, clutched
her head and pulled it back. Even with the contact
broken the taste of his mouth was still in hers, alive
with vibrant sensation, and his eyes glittered with the
unremitting conviction of that knowledge.

'Don't tell me all those days and nights together
meant nothing to you, Kathleen,' he said, his breath
mingling heatedly with hers. 'I could take you now and
you'd welcome me. Your whole body is crying out for
mine.'

'Yes. Yes, it is,' she blurted out, shaking with the
conflict between need and sanity. 'And you can take
me now. . .have me here on the grass if that's what
you want. I can't stop you. . .but it won't make me
stay with you afterwards, Morgan. You were right
about the colour of desire. It's a flame. . .and, like all
flames, it eventually goes out!'

She saw the certainty fade from his eyes, saw his

skin pale and tighten, and felt as sick as he began to look.

'You don't mean that, Kathleen,' he said, but the command in his voice was edged by pain.

She wavered for a moment, hating the hurt she was giving him. But the reality of their months together could not be ignored. 'How many times were you gone from my bed before I woke in the morning?' she hurled at him, goaded by all the pain he had given her and needing to exorcise it from her soul, to free herself from his dominance. Her voice gathered strength as the memories jabbed through her mind.

'When the flame was out, you walked away from me, Morgan. Without a word. Without a backward glance. You were always free to walk away. And you did. You didn't once think about what I thought or felt. It was all your way. And anything that got in your way, you dimissed out of hand. Even with the Eisteddfod, you didn't give me the courtesy of asking what I thought or felt. That didn't matter. Only your wants and needs ever mattered. You didn't care about me!'

He was shaking his head as if punch-drunk by her attack. 'That's not so. . .it wasn't like that, Kathleen. You were never out of my thoughts. You were all I——'

'No!' she screamed at him. 'You didn't care! Except in so far as I could be used for your purpose! I said I'd never call you Black Morgan. And I won't. But the reality. . .the truth, Morgan. . .is that you *are* black, because you blot out all other colours in your relentless drive to have your own way. No other shades exist for you. You *are* as black as the ace of spades!'

His face went chalk-white. He stared at her as if he was seeing the reflection of his own soul, and she felt the despair that drained him of all vitality. Only his eyes looked alive, and they were two glittering flames that danced to the agonies of hell.

'Say you don't mean that, Kathleen,' he rasped. 'You can't possibly mean that.'

She closed her eyes against the dark, mesmerising appeal of his. He was part of her. Always would be. And being separated from him had been like cutting off half of herself. But if she went back to him he would take all of her, immersing her in his life, his needs, his wants. . .and she would only ever be an appendage of him.

'You went with me, Kathleen. Always with me. Part of me.' His hands dragged through her hair to her shoulders, then slid slowly to her upper arms where they paused, his fingers working agitatedly over the soft flesh as if he knew he should release any hold on her but couldn't make himself do it. 'You've been the best part of me ever since you came into my home, Kathleen,' he said with a deep, raw intensity. 'You're the one good thing in my life. I need you. I have to have you. . .'

'Don't do this to me,' she begged, shaking her head against the relentless beat of his need. 'Let me go, Morgan,' she demanded in a desperate little voice.

'No. . .' It was a groan of despair. His fingers tightening around her arms.

Forcing his own will. . .always forcing no matter what words he mouthed. Sheer agony ripped through Kathleen's heart and mind. 'I have to be free of you!' she cried, tortured beyond bearing. Her eyes flashed up to his in bitter accusation and her voice rose in hysterical protest. 'Let me go! Leave me alone! You're no good for me, Morgan!'

His eyes seemed to dilate in horror. Disbelief and pure agony chased across his face. 'Kathleen. . .' It was a distraught whisper, spilling from lips that had lost all purpose. His grasp weakened. His hands fell away. There was suddenly a lifelessness about him that was not Morgan at all.

She was free to leave. He wasn't holding her any more. . .not with his eyes, or speech, or strength. Yet Kathleen hesitated, frightened by the eerie feeling that something terribly essential had died in him. The volatile energy, the aura of power that was so naturally his, the dynamic charisma of the man. . .it was as if they had all drained away, leaving an empty shell.

'Morgan?' It was a tentative question, prompted by the dreadful uncertainty fretting at her mind. Could she be wrong? Had he spoken the truth when he said she was more important to him than anything else?

'Do whatever you have to do. I will not hinder you.' His eyes were dull opaque darkness. He stepped back from her and turned to face out towards the ocean. 'I won't bother you again,' he said, and there was something in his voice that sent a shiver down her spine.

She couldn't go. She couldn't leave him here on the bluff. She had the frightening sensation that he might walk to the edge of the cliff if she turned her back on him. Might go further. . .just keep on walking, into nothingness.

She reached out and touched his arm. 'You have your music, Morgan,' she reminded him. That was what had been important to him. All he had cared about. Not her. If she pushed that back into his thoughts, he would be all right.

He shook his head, slowly and with resignation.

'*Lorna Doone* will be an enormous hit,' she said more urgently. 'Everyone will recognise that you're a truly great composer. You'll go on to bigger and better things. Just as you always wanted.'

He heaved a tired sigh and slanted her a mocking half-smile. 'There is no *Lorna Doone*. I did the only thing I could do. I destroyed it.'

Her heart stopped dead. Even when it fluttered into life again, she had difficulty drawing breath. 'What do you mean, you destroyed it?'

He shrugged. 'I burnt the music-sheets. Smashed the tapes.'

'Why?' she whispered, appalled at such wanton destruction. 'It was. . .exquisitely beautiful. It was. . .'

'What is *Lorna Doone* without you? It wasn't mine, Kathleen. It was ours,' he said, and he looked at her with a sick yearning that burrowed into her soul. 'When I realised that you didn't want it, and that what I'd done—what I am—had actually driven you away. . . I couldn't bear to have it around me. There was so much of you in it: what I wanted. . .what I'd longed for all my life. . .purity. . .innocence. . .' His mouth curled in bitter irony. 'Without you, what was it worth. And the answer to that was a blacker void than I've ever known before. Without you, my music is nothing. Worse. I hated it because it came between us. . .'

He shook his head and turned his gaze back to the ocean. 'I didn't even tell you how deeply you touched me. . .moved me. . .how much you meant to me,' he muttered, then made a harsh sound of self-contempt. 'I didn't know how much. . .until you'd gone.'

He shot her another twisted smile. 'Which shows how right you are, Kathleen. You're better off without a man like me. Black Morgan. That *is* the reality. . .the truth. You know it. . .and I know it. . .and it's well past time I paid for all my sins.'

For the first time since she had left him, Kathleen was racked with distressing uncertainties. Her mind was anguished with the knowledge that he had destroyed *Lorna*. And he had come after her. . .for her. . .and she meant more to him than the greatest music he had ever composed.

It was the last thing she had ever expected of him. And it shattered all her other knowledge of him. She felt she couldn't judge anything any more. Every instinct clamoured for a postponement of her decision, and even sharper was the intuitive feeling that she could not risk leaving him alone in this black frame of mind.

She dug her fingers into his arm. 'Would you mind helping me back to the farmhouse?' she asked. 'The path is rough. . .and my legs feel shaky.' Which was true enough. But her need for Morgan to accompany her had nothing to do with any physical disability.

A look of haunted suffering tightened his face. He swung around to support her, his arm reaching protectively around her waist and drawing her close so that her body was securely propped against his. 'I'm sorry, Kathleen,' he murmured in a low strained voice. 'I'll carry you if——'

'No. I can manage,' she cut in quickly, her cheeks flushing wildly at the automatic reaction of her body to his embrace.

She sensed the restraint he forced on himself as they began walking. Wretchedly self-conscious of her own weakness, Kathleen thought he had probably taken her swift refusal of his offer to carry her as a further rejection. But it was too late to recant. And it would only torment them both to be any closer than they were now.

As he carefully matched his step to hers, Kathleen remembered the tenderness he had shown her that first night when he had seen the scars on her legs, the way he had cradled her in his arms and sworn she would have every chance to fulfil her dream. And he had done his best. He would have made her a recording star with *Lorna Doone*. And he had said she could sing at the Eisteddfod next year.

Perhaps she had misjudged him. It was certainly possible. If she had spoken up more, told him what she was feeling, forced him to understand that he was taking too much for granted. . .not been so stifled by her dependence on him for everything! Perhaps he was not as black as she had painted him.

Could they start over again now? Would he listen? Did he truly love her. . .as she loved him?

Kathleen trembled from the sheer force of her need to believe that their relationship could have the closeness she craved, the mutual love and understanding that would be better than any dream.

As the full impact of what she was thinking hit her, she faltered in her step. Morgan reacted instantly, misunderstanding the reason for her shaky hesitation. He swooped and lifted her up in his arms, not giving her any time to protest.

'You can trust me to carry you, Kathleen,' he said harshly, and strode on, his features grimly set, his eyes focused steadily on the far distance like an old-time clipper captain whose boat was inexorably bearing down on hull-tearing rocks.

Kathleen couldn't resist the temptation to wind her arms around his neck and burrow her face into the warmth of his throat. She felt the corded muscles tighten, sensed his pulse quicken, and knew his desire for her was unabated, that it was banked behind a rigid control which would take him away from her. . .if she didn't stop him.

Lucille Millot had apparently been keeping an eye

on Kathleen's visitor. She opened the front door of the farmhouse before Morgan reached it. There was a rapid exchange in French that Kathleen did not follow, but Lucille stood back and Morgan headed straight for the staircase, obviously intent on taking her up to her room.

It was an awkward exercise, carrying her up the stairs, but Kathleen did not ask him to put her down. She did not have to be told why he chose to take her as far as her room instead of placing her on the nearest chair. She knew intuitively that he was feeling what she herself felt. He was holding on to this last semblance of togetherness as long as he could, putting off the moment when they had to confront parting from each other.

He mounted each stair with a reluctance which grew more prolonged as he neared the top. His arms tightened around her in blind, driven possessiveness. He paused at her door for long moments before opening it, then leaned against it for even longer moments when he shut it behind him. When he finally pushed himself to cross the room to the bed he moved slowly, stiffly, as if each footstep was an act of will-power alone.

His breathing was harsh as he laid her gently on the soft quilt. His eyes evaded hers until he tried to pull away and Kathleen clung to him, not letting him go. Then he looked at her with such deep anguish that there was no decision to make. She could not stop the words tumbling from her heart.

'I love you, Morgan. And I don't want to live without you. I need you in my life too. If there is some way we can work it out. . .so that we can be together. . .'

He closed his eyes tight. His chest heaved several

times before he opened them again to search hers in frantic need. 'Kathleen, I don't want to hurt you. Not in any way. I don't know how to be. . .what you want me to be. I do everything wrong. . .'

'Tell me that you love me,' she pleaded huskily.

'I love you.' He groaned, and pressed slow, infinitely hungry kisses all around her face, almost as if he dared not touch her lips yet. But even the sensation of his breath against her skin was enough to make her quiver with pleasure. 'I love you with all that I am, all that I'll ever be,' he said thickly. 'And I ache for you to be part of me again, Kathleen. I'm nothing without you. You're the music of my life. Everything.'

'I thought you were only using me,' she whispered. 'That I was just a means to an end. And when it ended. . . I didn't know if I could survive that, Morgan.'

He gathered her up and held her tightly to him, rocking both of them in an agonised assurance that they would never be parted again. He rubbed his cheek over her hair like a wounded animal in desperate need of soothing, and he spoke in broken bursts of speech that were pushed from the torment of his soul.

'The songs I wrote for John Ridd: they were what you made me feel, Kathleen. The wonder of you—not Lorna, you—and I never wanted it to end. Never. I wouldn't have thought of marrying you if I hadn't expected us to stay together. For the rest of our lives.'

So she had been wrong about that too, Kathleen thought in shuddering relief. The timing might have been pure show business, but the intent of marriage had not been cynical.

'Tell me how to do it right. Tell me what you want. What would make you happy, Kathleen?' he begged, and she felt the violent surge of purpose in him, and exulted in the power that she knew was hers now. . .the power to fire him with new life and ambition.

She pulled away, wanting to see his face, his eyes, and her heart turned over at the burning desire and adoration that looked back at her. 'I'd like to be your wife, Morgan,' she said, any doubts about his feelings for her seared away by the naked intensity of his emotion.

His reply was swift, as if he feared she might change her mind. 'I'll have it arranged. For tomorrow. . .'

'It doesn't matter when. I'll never leave you, Morgan,' she said softly, deeply moved by his need for her. 'As long as you love me and want me, I'll be beside you.'

He touched her face, caressing her fine skin with a tenderness that made her tremble with a strange new excitement. She turned her head to kiss his fingers. He made some unintelligible sound, and her eyes lifted to his in open invitation to take whatever he wanted of her.

'I love you,' she whispered. 'Please. . .kiss me.'

Desire, the drive to possess—she had known that from him, but there was something totally different in the way Morgan kissed her now. . .an awareness of more than a physical mingling. It heightened their senses, sharpened them to a poignancy that could only be answerable by every possible intimacy. Any barrier between them was intolerable.

His hands shook as he stripped away her clothes, and he reacted with intense sensitivity when she helped him from his. He took her hands and thrust them away from him, holding them down on the bed. 'Don't touch me, my darling. I'll lose control. And I want to love you. I want to show you. . .'

'No, Morgan. No control. I need to feel you too,' she pleaded, aching for the pleasure of holding him and having him inside her.

'Kathleen, you don't know. . .' he protested.

'I want to know,' she replied with all the wild passion building within her. 'I want you. . .any way you are, Morgan. It's you. . .and I love you.'

His breathing quickened even as he released her hands, and when she reached out her arms for him he moved over her with a fierce, deliberate eroticism that sent sharp pangs of desire racing through her. She writhed with voluptuous excitement and exulted in every straining muscle of his body as he strove to hold back, to savour the sensual delight of her soft femininity. The heat and the power of his tight male flesh was such a heady pleasure that she barely knew what she was doing as she raked her hands down his back. All she could think of was that he was hers. . .truly hers. . .and she could never have enough of him.

He cried out as if in unbearable torment and the feverish trail of his kisses came to an abrupt halt. He drew away from her grasp, lifted her body to his and drove inside her with a frenzied need that had her arching up in a wild agony-joy. She heard herself cry out words of exultant possession as Morgan sent surges of intense sensation through her, heard him make hoarse responses to her demands, but the pleasure of uninhibited speech was only a ripple of delight swirling over the fierce storm of need that rocked their bodies in a rhythm of violent urgency.

Words disintegrated into incoherent sounds as they searched for the ecstatic release that had slipped beyond their control. Breathing hurt. Her muscles disobeyed all demands, tightening to unendurable want under the frantic thrusting need of his body. She threshed wildly from side to side. His arms dug under her, half lifting her from the bed, pressing her against every inch of his body, savouring every fragment of contact.

She could not move. Morgan was slowly crushing her as he drove towards his final climax. Her mouth found the tender skin near his throat and she sucked on it in mindless desperation for him. He made a harsh animal sound and somehow she found the strength to wrap her legs around him, urging him into a wilder frenzy of possession.

Something snapped in Kathleen's head. Something so wonderful, so beautiful; a bliss, a glow, an effusion so sweet. She surrendered to Morgan's raging climax, limp in his arms as he stole exquisite pleasure from her body. She vaguely heard him cry out her name and, like a mantra that he could not stop reciting over and over again, 'I love you. . . I love you. . . I love you. . .'

He kissed her as though she was the most precious thing in the world. He wrapped her in his arms. He locked her legs to his. He touched her as if he needed to keep affirming that she was real and shuddered with pleasure when Kathleen found strength enough to move contentedly against him. She slid her arm around his back and pressed him closer to her. He sighed and relaxed at last into peaceful satisfaction.

She sensed that he was going to speak, and reached up to run a finger over his lips. Their eyes met, and there was no need for speech. It was enough to be together. There had been too much talk. Too much misunderstanding. Tomorrow they could talk. This was a time for loving, and letting the love seep slowly into their souls. . .warm. . .secure. . .inviolable. . .no matter what the future held for them.

CHAPTER TWELVE

THERE was nothing black about Morgan the next day. He emanated the same volatile energy that had made such an impact on Kathleen at their first meeting, but it was pure white happiness that radiated from him. . .blazed from him in a glow that encompassed Kathleen so totally that sometimes she caught her breath at the incredible change in him. But in another way he hadn't changed at all. From the moment they had risen he had been bursting with plans and making arrangements at a pace that was almost bewildering.

'But how can we get married here?' she asked, dazed by the fire of Morgan's determination.

He grinned, his eyes dancing at her innocence. 'My darling girl, if you've got enough money, you can do just about anything. And I've had a fair amount of practice at it. All we need for the civil ceremoy are two things. Our birth certificates and our residential certificates. Madame Desfarges cleared the way, and I came prepared. Hell-bent on having you any way I could. And I will. Today we are going to be married. Which will put the issue permanently beyond doubt.'

Kathleen shook her head in bemusement. 'I still don't know how you convinced Madame to co-operate with you.'

Morgan drew her into his arms. 'I doubt she's ever seen a man as desperate as I was, my love. And she was very concerned about you. The Millots informed her that you hadn't sung a note since you'd been here. When I gave my solemn word I'd do nothing to interfere with your chosen career, and everything to support it, she decided it was up to you if you wanted me in your life or not.'

She wound her arms around his neck, her blue eyes shining with love for him. 'I want you,' she said, and kissed him with sufficient fervour to prove it to his satisfaction.

Morgan dragged in a deep breath. 'I'm not taking you back to bed,' he said decisively. 'I'm taking you to the village. Marriage before pleasure, Kathleen Mavourney. And besides getting legally married, we've got to see the priest to line up a church wedding too. We have to wait three weeks for that. When we're in Paris for the Eisteddfod, we'll buy you the most beautiful wedding dress we can find. Then we'll come back here and get married again.'

'Don't I have any say in this, Morgan Llewellyn?' she demanded archly.

He checked himself, searching her eyes intently. 'Not really,' he said slowly. 'But if that's not what you want, you only have to speak. . .'

'And you'll find some other way of accomplishing it.' She laughed and stroked his cheek with soothing tenderness. 'I was only teasing you. It is what I want, Morgan.'

His face relaxed into an indulgent smile. 'Any time you don't like what I do, just tell me, Kathleen. One thing I have got straightened out in my life is my priorities. And more important than anything else is to keep you happy with me.'

'I'm deliriously happy,' she assured him.

But there was one little niggle in the back of her mind. Quite a big niggle in fact. She hated the thought that *Lorna Doone* had been destroyed. While the sacrifice of his music had proved his love for her beyond a shadow of doubt, Kathleen couldn't bear it to be lost. It was part of them. They had made it together. And she couldn't accept such a sacrifice from Morgan.

Surely he could remember most of it? It couldn't be entirely gone from his mind. And she could help him. She hadn't forgotten any of Lorna's songs. And she wanted to sing Lorna for him. But now wasn't the right time to approach that problem. Perhaps when they went home. . .

'I rang Tibbet this morning,' Morgan told her as he walked her very purposefully from the farmhouse to the car—a black Porsche which was a new acquisition since she had left the Hermitage.

She glanced up at him enquiringly.

His mouth quirked. 'I had to tell her you were coming home with me. As Mrs Llewellyn. It was a matter of self-protection. I've been getting the cold shoulder and the stiff upper lip from the whole staff. It was unbearable. I nearly lost my temper with them. Now I'm assured of a warm welcome with my new bride.'

A delicious warmth ran through Kathleen. 'I'm so glad to be going back. They were all so terribly nice to me.'

Morgan hugged her closer to him. 'Which was more than I was. But I swear I'll make it up to you, Kathleen. And meanwhile, Tibbet said to pass on congratulations and best wishes from all the staff. I had the impression that she barely restrained herself from saying, "and not before time".'

Kathleen laughed and snuggled her head on to his shoulder. 'I guess they knew I loved you.'

Morgan dropped a kiss on her hair. 'I don't think they had much doubt about where you stood with me after you left that morning. I'm afraid I put them all through a close approximation to the Spanish Inquisition. I hope I'm now forgiven.'

They drove to Pont-Croix and completed all the formalities for the civil marriage to take place. Which it did. Without any pomp or ceremony. But that didn't matter at all. The love in Morgan's eyes was all Kathleen wanted. However, Morgan took much satisfaction in collecting the marriage certificate and stowing it carefully in her handbag.

'Well, Mrs Llewellyn,' he said triumphantly, 'we are now officially on our honeymoon. And we have permission from your formidable teacher to spend a few more days at the farmhouse to get your voice into appropriate working order. We could go somewhere else if you like, but I might remind you it's the closest place and I feel like an awful lot of loving. . .'

'Definitely the farmhouse,' Kathleen agreed, elated by his need for her. 'But there's one thing I want to do first. . .if you don't mind.'

'Whatever. . .' he said grandly.

She flicked him an anxious glance. 'I'd like to send a postcard to Sister Cecily. Would you mind, Morgan?'

'The Little Scourge of My Life,' he mused softly. 'Yes. Why not? We owe it to her. And a lot more besides.'

It was a simple message they sent.

> Morgan and I were married today. Two people could not be more happy. Morgan concedes to you over the music. All our love.
>   Kathleen.

In the days that followed Kathleen hesitated to bring up the subject of *Lorna Doone* in case it pained Morgan to remember it. Unfortunately she could not keep burying it. She wanted Morgan to be as happy as she was. And she knew how important *Lorna Doone* had been to him. They were having a luncheon picnic on top of the bluff when she finally screwed up the courage to share her concern about the music with him.

He stared out at the ocean for a long time before answering. 'No. Let it go, Kathleen. I couldn't remember it all and I don't want to work through every note again. That would be torture. And if I didn't get every note exactly right. . . No, I'll compose other music for your voice. Something specially for you. Not for me.'

'What about. . .for us?' she asked quietly.

He dragged his gaze away from the ocean and looked at her, his eyes full of dark emotions. 'I don't want any bad memories. This is a new start for us, Kathleen. I couldn't bear for it to be tarnished in any way. No doubts. No fears. Nothing that could come between us.'

Kathleen didn't argue. She remembered Sister Cecily saying her worst fault was that she argued too much—even though that wasn't true. She sensed that the wounds from that music were still too raw for Morgan to contemplate what she had asked. But she hoped one day he would reconsider.

'Whatever you want,' she said softly. 'When the time is right, it will come back to you.'

She smiled at him, and when she saw the happy warmth creep back into his eyes she leaned forward to kiss him, to give him all the love he craved from her.

The days passed all too quickly and Madame Desfarges telephoned to say—with some asperity—that it was time Kathleen was back in London if she was to have any hope of winning the competition. No matter what happened, life must go on. Judges judged competitions on the performance of the performers, and not on how happy they were.

They set off for home the next morning. Kathleen fell asleep on the last leg of the journey and when Morgan woke her she was surprised to see they were not at the Hermitage at all, but parked just outside the convent gates where she had said goodbye to Sister Cecily on that fateful afternoon so long ago.

'I was thinking of her while you slept. I figured we should thank her in person,' he explained with a whimsical smile.

Kathleen leaned over and hugged him. 'That was a wonderful thought, Morgan. I do so love you.'

'Then I have my reward,' he said, and very nearly changed her mind by kissing her.

However, the convent beckoned, and eventually they walked up the path to the front door with the eager step of happy anticipation, their arms around each other's waists, their faces glowing with the love they could now share with their old teacher.

Kathleen rang the bell.

One of the younger nuns answered the summons and her face stiffened with shock when she recognised Kathleen.

'Don't look so surprised, Sister,' Kathleen half laughed. 'This is my husband, Morgan Llewellyn. I wrote to Sister Cecily that we were married, and we've come to see her.'

'Mr Llewellyn,' the nun acknowledged belatedly, still looking quite disturbed by the impromptu visit.

'Don't let us worry you, Sister,' Kathleen said brightly. 'We'll just go straight through to the music wing.'

An arm fluttered out as Kathleen stepped forward. 'No. . .' The nun looked even more distressed as she struggled to explain herself. 'Kathleen, I. . . I think you. . .and Mr Llewellyn. . .should see Mother Superior first. Please. . .if you'd wait a moment.'

She hurried off along the hallway, leaving Kathleen and Morgan to raise quizzical eyebrows at each other. Kathleen shrugged. 'It is only courtesy.'

Morgan nodded. 'Is it still the same old tartar, Mother Mary Joesph?'

Kathleen grinned. 'You had some run-ins with her?'

Morgan sighed. 'Quite a few private sessions in her office. I wasn't the best-behaved kid in the class.'

They fell silent as the nun hastened back to them. 'If you will come with me,' she beckoned, 'Mother Superior will see you now.'

They followed her along a corridor until she opened a door and ushered Kathleen and Morgan through to the inner sanctum of convent authority. Mother Mary Joseph was already on her feet to greet them. Kathleen had the fleeting impression that the woman seemed much older than she remembered. How long had she been away from the convent? Perhaps time could play tricks like that.

'It is good to see both of you. And together.' A ghost of a smile took the stiffness from her lips. 'Please sit down. I have something to give you. . .and something to tell you.'

An eerie sense of premonition ran down Kathleen's spine. She threw a sharp glance at Morgan as she settled on one of the chairs, but he was observing the elderly nun who slowly and wearily sank into the chair behind her desk. She opened a drawer and drew out a large cardboard box. She pushed it across the desk-top towards Morgan.

'This is yours, Morgan, and perhaps you would like

o take it back now,' she said with a touch of sad
esignation.

'Mine?' Morgan reached over and took the box. He
ifted off the lid in puzzled curiosity. On top of a large
tack of photocopied music-sheets were a letter and a
ape.

He quickly scanned the letter and passed it to
Kathleen with an ironic shake of his head. It was
written on the Hermitage stationery and was addressed
o Sister Cecily. It read,

> You will recall that you spoke of Mr Llewellyn's
> unfulfilled talent when you visited the Hermitage.
> You will remember our agreement. Therefore I am
> sending this music to you for your satisfaction. It is
> the complete score of *Lorna Doone*. The tape is a
> recording of the songs written for Lorna and sung by
> Miss Mavourney. I feel sure that this will measure
> up to your standards of excellence.

It was signed 'Florence Tibbet'.

'That's incredible!' Kathleen murmured. 'The music
s all here. It doesn't have to be recomposed from
memory. But Tibbet? How could she know that. . .or
lid Sister Cecily ask her?' It seemed such an extra-
ordinary thing to do—to go behind Morgan's back—
'et the little nun might have woven her powerful magic
n Tibbet's mind as well as in Morgan's and her own.

'She showed Sister Cecily around the Hermitage. No
loubt they had an interesting conversation. And they
vould understand each other perfectly,' Morgan said
lrily. 'Tibbet always knows everything. And has a fine
land at anticipation as well. I think. . .more a safe-
uard against what I might do. . .and did. And who
etter to entrust it to?'

'Thank heaven she did it anyway!' Kathleen

breathed in relief—the music wasn't lost after all—bu
still an uneasy feeling wormed through her heart. Why
had Mother Superior given the parcel to Morgan'
Where was Sister Cecily?

She looked searchingly at the elderly nun and wa
dismayed to see tears filming her eyes. There wa
something wrong. . .badly wrong. 'She isn't well, i
she?' Kathleen asked anxiously.

'I'm afraid not, my dear.' She took a large whit
handkerchief from the voluminous pocket in her nun'
habit and wiped her eyes. 'This is going to be a shoc
to you. As it has been to all of us. Siste
Cecily. . .died. . .in her sleep. . .two nights ago. Th
tape. . .your music, Morgan. . .and Kathleen's sing
ing. . .gave her a great deal of pleasure. As did th
news of your marriage. It was. . . I think. . .the cul
mination of her life's work. She died. . .very
peacefully.'

'Died. . .' Kathleen's shock was too deep to say any
more. She had thought, perhaps unwell, possibly very
ill, but not. . .dead. Her friend. . .her teacher. . .he
mentor. . .that little woman who had stood by her fo
so long and given so much. . .

Tears welled into her eyes and rolled unheede
down her cheeks. Morgan's hand came across and
grasped hers hard, squeezing warmly.

'How did it happen?' Morgan asked, and there wa
a strained note in his voice as he added, 'Was there
anything we could have done?'

'No. You gave her what she most wanted, Morgan
You and Kathleen, together. There was no illness
Nothing that could have been fixed. . .or prevented
Sister Cecily was. . .not young. Who knows why some
one dies? Perhaps her mission in this life had been
completed. I think, for her, that's how it was.'

Morgan's hand gripped Kathleen's tightly. 'I wish I ould have thanked her. . .for all she had done for me. never did. Not once in all my life. I never thanked er.'

Mother Superior shook her head. 'Don't have any egrets, Morgan. Sister Cecily did not need to be anked. Of all the pupils she taught over the years, ou were the most special to her. . .you and Kathleen. ut most especially you, Morgan. She preferred to each boys. And the fact that you finally composed usic that was commensurate with your talent. . .you ere the return of the Prodigal Son. You lived in her eart. . .in her prayers. You were always in her mind. n a spiritual sense, both of you. . .were like children he had given birth to. . .'

Tears glistened in her eyes again and she paused a oment to regather her composure. 'She was not a ood nun. She had no idea of the concept of obedience. nd always the need. . .the drive for perfection. et. . . I shall miss her more than anyone else I've ver known. It's like the passing of an era. . .the assing of an age. I doubt the world will ever see her ke again.'

Morgan bowed his head. 'Is there anything I can o?'

'Go on with what you have started, my dear. She as so proud of your *Lorna Doone*. She played the ape to all of us. We were all proud of you.'

'I'm glad. . .that she heard it. . .that she new. . .that she was pleased enough with the music want to share it with you.'

Kathleen took a deep breath and forced the words he wanted to say past the lump in her throat. 'Is it ossible. . .to pay my last respects. . .in the chapel?'

'Yes, Kathleen. The Requiem Mass is to be held in

the morning. Sister is there. And she would be glad i
you were to say a prayer for her.'

'Thank you, Mother. I would like that.'

She turned a beseeching look to Morgan who ros
instantly to his feet, his arm encircling her shoulders t
help her up.

The elderly nun pushed herself up from her chai
'I'll take you there myself.'

Morgan handed Kathleen his handkerchief and sh
tried to mop up her tears as they walked the lon
echoing corridors. Memories kept crowding in on her
and only the strength of Morgan's support stopped he
from breaking down altogether.

The sweet smell of freesias permeated the chapel
Sister Cecily had always liked them. A littl
flower. . .but one whose strong scent insisted on no
being ignored. Power, Kathleen thought, and coul
not hold back a rush of tears.

The casket, set up in state in front of the altar, wa
white. And looked very small. She might have bee
little in physical stature, Kathleen thought, but in ever
other way Sister Cecily had been a giant. Mothe
Superior was right: the passing of an era. . .the passin
of an age.

She didn't look old at all. She almost looke
young. . .serene. . .peaceful. Give us your blessing
Sister, Kathleen prayed. You brought us together wit
your power. And we will celebrate it with our live
together.

She looked up at Morgan and there were tears in hi
eyes. 'She was one hell of a person, Kathleen,' he sai
grimly. 'Apart from you, she meant more to me tha
anyone else in my life. I wish. . .' He shook his head
'No. . .it's all right. She knew when she brought u

gether. She held out the last chance to me. . .and
ank God I took it!'

'It was my chance too, Morgan,' Kathleen whis-
ered, and their eyes met in deep and mutual under-
anding of the power the little nun had wielded on
eir behalf.

'We'll do *Lorna Doone* for her,' Morgan said.

'Yes. She started it. It's hers, as well as ours.'

And their pain mingled with a strong burgeoning of
ve. The music would go on—the music Sister Cecily
d fought for. . .the music of their lives. Nothing
uld stop it now. The power was in their hands. . .in
eir hearts. . .and minds. . .and souls. The little nun
d taught them well.

AUTHOR'S NOTE

SHOULD any readers be interested, and the book of
Lorna Doone is not available to them through local
libraries, Lorna did not die from the wound inflicted
on her by Carver on her wedding day. To quote John
Ridd's words at the end of the book:

> Of Lorna, of my lifelong darling, of my more
> and more loved wife, I will not talk; for it is not
> seemly, that a man should exalt his pride. Year by
> year her beauty grows, with the growth of goodness,
> kindness, and true happiness—above all with loving.

Lorna Doone—A Romance of Exmoor—written by
R. D. Blackmore—first published in 1869—sub-
sequently published in 1913 as a 'World Classic'.

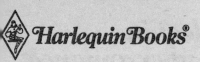
◆ *Harlequin Books*®

GREAT NEWS . . .
HARLEQUIN UNVEILS NEW SHIPPING PLANS

For the convenience of customers, Harlequin has announced that Harlequin romances will now be available in stores at these convenient times each month*:

Harlequin Presents, American Romance, Historical, Intrigue:

> May titles: April 10
> June titles: May 8
> July titles: June 5
> August titles: July 10

Harlequin Romance, Superromance, Temptation, Regency Romance:

> May titles: April 24
> June titles: May 22
> July titles: June 19
> August titles: July 24

We hope this new schedule is convenient for you.

With only two trips each month to your local bookseller, you'll never miss any of your favorite authors!

*Please note: There may be slight variations in on-sale dates in your area due to differences in shipping and handling.
*Applicable to U.S. only.

HDATES-RR

Harlequin Superromance®

Available in Superromance this month
#462—STARLIT PROMISE

STARLIT PROMISE is a deeply moving story of a
woman coming to terms with her grief and gradually
opening her heart to life and love.

Author Petra Holland sets the scene beautifully, never
allowing her heroine to become mired in self-pity. It
is a story that will touch your heart and leave you
celebrating the strength of the human spirit.

Available wherever Harlequin books
are sold.

STARLIT-A

HARLEQUIN
Romance

**This September, travel to England
with Harlequin Romance
FIRST CLASS title #3149,
ROSES HAVE THORNS
by Betty Neels**

It was Radolf Nauta's fault that Sarah lost her job at the hospital and was forced to look elsewhere for a living. So she wasn't particulary pleased to meet him again in a totally different environment. Not that he seemed disposed to be gracious to her: arrogant, opinionated and entirely too sure of himself, Radolf was just the sort of man Sarah disliked most. And yet, the more she saw of him, the more she found herself wondering what he really thought about her—which was stupid, because he was the last man on earth she could ever love....

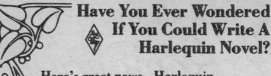

Have You Ever Wondered If You Could Write A Harlequin Novel?

Here's great news—Harlequin is offering a series of cassette tapes to help you do just that. Written by Harlequin editors, these tapes give practical advice on how to make your characters—and your story—come alive. There's a tape for each contemporary romance series Harlequin publishes.

Mail order only

All sales final

✂ -

Harlequin Superromance®

CHILDREN OF THE HEART
by Sally Garrett

Available this month

Romance readers the world over have wept and
rejoiced over Sally Garrett's heartwarming stories of
love, caring and commitment. In her new novel,
Children of the Heart, Sally once again weaves a story
that will touch your most tender emotions.

You'll be moved to tears of joy

Nearly two hundred children have passed through
Trenance McKay's foster home. But after her husband
leaves her, Trenance knows she'll always have to
struggle alone. No man could have enough room in his
heart both for Trenance and for so many needy
children. Max Tulley, news anchor for KSPO TV is
willing to try, but how long can his love last?

"Sally Garrett does some of the best character studies
in the genre and will not disappoint her fans."
Romantic Times

**Look for *Children of the Heart* wherever
Harlequin Romance novels are sold.**   SCH

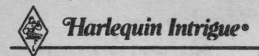

Trust No One...

When you are outwitting a cunning killer, confronting dark secrets or unmasking a devious imposter, it's hard to know whom to trust. Strong arms reach out to embrace you—but are they a safe harbor...or a tiger's den?

When you're on the run, do you dare to fall in love?

For heart-stopping suspense and heart-stirring romance, read Harlequin Intrigue. Two new titles each month.

HARLEQUIN INTRIGUE—where you can expect the unexpected.